DECISION

When Sister Clare Summers accompanies a badly injured patient to his home in France she believes herself to be in love. Why should the arrogant Dr Alain Duval be so determined to make her doubt this belief?

DECISION
FOR A NURSE

BY

JEAN EVANS

MILLS & BOON LIMITED
London · Sydney · Toronto

First published in Great Britain 1982
by Mills & Boon Limited, 15–16 Brook's Mews,
London W1A 1DR

ISBN 0 263 74079 X

Set in 11 on 12 pt Linotron Times
03/1182

Photoset by Rowland Phototypesetting Ltd
Bury St Edmunds, Suffolk
Made and printed in Great Britain by
Richard Clay (The Chaucer Press) Ltd
Bungay, Suffolk

CHAPTER ONE

CLARE Summers' shoes squeaked softly as she made her way along Nightingale Ward, pausing at the foot of each bed to check the chart which was clipped to the rail and making sure that the occupants were asleep.

A pale overhead light cast shadows onto her face, emphasising its striking contours beneath the white frilled cap. There was competence as well as compassion in her grey eyes and her mouth still bore the slightly upward curve of generous good humour, even though at this moment she felt both physically and mentally exhausted.

It had been a long night and there was still a long way to go before she handed over to the day staff at eight and finally drove to the small flat she had been lucky enough to find at the other end of town. St Mary's boasted a rather ancient but very nice Nurses' Home, but somehow she had clung to a style of independence which had been thrust upon her rather than chosen. She enjoyed the company of the people she worked with, but it was good to be able to escape at the end of the day from the smell of antiseptics and shop talk.

She paused again as the figure in the bed moved restlessly. 'Hullo, Mr Reynolds, can't you sleep?'

Sam Reynolds felt vaguely ashamed of the feeling of relief the sight of her slim, navy-blue clad figure gave him. He moved his head against the pillows, leaving his grey hair standing on end. ''Fraid not, Sister. I've been lying here for hours.'

'But why didn't you call me?'

'Didn't want to be a damn nuisance. You girls are rushed off your feet.'

'We're never *too* busy. I've told you that before. Shall I see if I can make you more comfortable? If I didn't know better I'd say you'd been fighting with those pillows.' Supporting him gently she re-arranged them behind him and he settled back, sighing.

'Aye, that's better.'

She smiled. Nurses weren't supposed to have their favourites but it was easy to become attached to some patients. 'Are you in pain? Can I get you something?'

'No, I'm fine, at least it's nothing to bother about. Got to expect a twinge or two. Besides, you've got enough on your hands as it is.' He nodded the length of the ward. 'Filled up, hasn't it, since I came in?'

'Yes it has, but that's the way it goes. Sometimes we have empty beds for days, then they fill up almost before you can turn round.' She wrote on the chart and returned it to its clip. 'Are you sure I can't get you anything? How about a cup of tea? It might help and Staff and I were just about to have one anyway.'

'Well that would be very nice, if it's all right. Don't want to get you lasses into trouble.'

'Oh, there's no chance of that, I promise you. Staff,' she beckoned the girl in a pale mauve uniform. 'Do you think we might manage an extra cup of tea for Mr Reynolds?'

'Sure, I don't see why not, Sister.' Kathy O'Donnell smiled. 'Shall I see to it now, while we're quiet?'

'If you wouldn't mind. We can't have Mr Reynolds lying awake half the night, can we?'

'They reckon tea keeps you awake. I never found it did,' he confided as she tucked the sheets loosely round him and automatically felt for his pulse.

She nodded approvingly. 'Well that's fine. You're doing very well you know. Doctor is very pleased with that hip of yours. I should think you'll be ready to leave us fairly soon.'

'Do you think so, Sister?'

'A few more days I'm sure and you'll be as good as new, you know. You'll be able to walk quite normally and without any pain.'

His face clouded and the reaction surprised her. 'That's what I miss really, you see, being cooped up here like. Only I tend to wander round the house a bit at nights when I can't sleep. Make myself a cup of tea, sit and read. Started after the missus died. Silly really, I always used to reckon she was a great lump of a thing, taking up more than her fair share of the bed.' His voice trailed away. 'Funny though, I can't seem to settle without her there. Something to warm my feet on.' He broke off, laughing, but she heard the faint catch in his voice. 'Daft, ain't it?'

She shook her head and she could feel the trembling of his hand as he gripped hers. 'No, I don't think it's daft, Mr Reynolds. As a matter of fact I know what you mean.'

'What, a young thing like you? I wouldn't have thought you'd have many sleepless nights, not the way you're on your feet all day.'

'Well as a matter of fact I've done a bit of floor walking myself, after my parents were killed in a car crash.'

'Is that right? Well it just shows you never know what other people's troubles are, do you, Sister? And here am I, too wrapped up in my own.'

'Oh, it was a long time ago now. Not that you ever forget, of course, but after a while it doesn't hurt quite so much does it, and I suppose we have to get on with the business of living.'

'Aye, but it's not so easy 'til you've got the hang of it.'

'No, it's not.' She smiled, recognising the embarrassment he felt, as if aware that he had revealed feelings usually kept hidden, and she changed the subject. 'It's been snowing again, quite hard.'

'I know, I've been watching it. I like snow, makes everything look nice and clean and new.'

'So do I. Unfortunately it means our Casualty Department will be rushed off their feet. We always hate this time of year for the accidents it causes.'

'Aye,' he murmured, reflectively. 'I dare say it won't be much of a Christmas for some.'

'What will you be doing? You've a family haven't you?'

'That's right, a daughter. She's asked me over to stay, but I shan't bother. She's her hands full enough with the two children to want to be bothering about me.'

'Now I'm sure that's not true.' The defensive note in his voice hadn't gone unnoticed. 'She obviously thinks enough of you to take the trouble to invite you, and are you really being fair to those grandchildren of yours?'

'I don't see what you're getting at, Sister.'

'Well, independence is all very well, Mr Reynolds, but don't you think you might be depriving them of a lot of fun by refusing to share their Christmas with them? There's often a great bond of affection between the very young and the elderly you know.' Her face clouded momentarily. 'I adored my own gran. She brought me up after my parents died, at least for a while. I remember I cried for days when she sent me away to school.'

'Sent you away?' He snorted. 'Can't say I see much love in that.'

'Ah yes, but you see she lived in Scotland and her cottage was so remote that I scarcely saw another child from one week to the next apart from in the tiny school, and then there were only ten of us and we all went our separate ways at the end of the day. Of course I was blissfully happy, but she had the sense to see that she wouldn't be there for ever and sooner or later I was going to have to go out into the big wide world and get myself a job. So you see, sending me away was a kindness. Not that I appreciated it at the time, that came later, but those years I spent with her were very special. So you see, you may still have something to offer.'

He studied her and grinned. 'I have the feeling you're trying to tell me something, Sister.'

'Well, I'm asking you to reconsider, that's all.' She helped him to sit up as Kathy O'Donnell appeared with his cup of tea.

'Here we are then. No sugar, just the way you like it, and I've put a biscuit in the saucer just to help it down. It's lucky for them as don't have to diet,' she winked. 'Yours is ready when you are, Sister.'

'Thank you, Staff. I'll be along just as soon as I've checked the rest of the patients.'

Kathy put the cup on the locker. 'And what are you doing for Christmas, Mr Reynolds?'

Walking away, Clare smiled to herself as she heard him answer. 'Oh, I'll be going to my daughter. I reckon she'll need some help to keep those two youngsters of hers in order. The young don't seem to have the knack these days somehow . . .'

Old Sam Reynolds still had a lot to offer, Clare thought. Perhaps, just temporarily, he had lost sight of the fact.

In the office she poured tea and sat back with a sigh of relief to enjoy it. The report book lay open on the desk in front of her, awaiting her attention. 'Have you been for your meal yet, Staff?' She consulted her watch but the pretty Irish girl shook her head.

'No, Sister, thank you very much. Shepherd's pie and treacle sponge can cause havoc with a girl's diet, and besides,' she patted her waistline, 'I'm still doing penance for yesterday's steak and kidney pudding. The trouble is, I'm very firm in my intentions but I've no resistance, you see.'

Clare grinned. 'Well to be perfectly honest, steak and kidney pud is one thing I've no difficulty in resisting, but I suppose I'm lucky.'

'Yes, indeed you are. But why don't you go for your meal now, Sister? Everything's quiet. Ah, now wouldn't you just know it,' she groaned as the blue flashing lights of an ambulance signalled its approach at Casualty. Watching from the window she nodded. 'I shouldn't have spoken so soon. Still, it may not be for Nightingale.'

Clare pulled the report book towards her, tapping her pen against her teeth. 'We don't have a spare bed anyway, not until tomorrow when young Keith Raymond goes home, apart from the side ward.' She mused, frowning, over the pages. 'Francis Ward is full too. Look, I think we'd better check the side ward just in case Casualty ring through.' Draining her cup she got to her feet, easing the wide belt spanning her waist. 'I'll pop down to the cafeteria and get a sandwich or something. I didn't get a chance to eat before I came on duty, not when I saw that snow. It took me an extra half an hour to get here as it was.'

'I'll see to it, Sister,' Kathy was already at the door. 'Whatever it is, Casualty are going to be some time anyway.'

Clare nodded, making her way from the small office out into the corridor and down the stairs towards the hospital cafeteria. For some reason she felt a sudden, strange reluctance to leave the ward and hesitated on the stairs, only to pull herself up with a jerk. 'This is ridiculous,' she chided herself. 'I shan't be away for more than ten minutes. Why get so jumpy just because an admission has come in? It happens all the time.'

At this hour of the night she knew the cafeteria would probably be almost empty. Staff tended to take their meals erratically, whenever there was a brief lull on the wards rather than at set times. In fact it hadn't been unknown for them to be missed altogether if they were particularly rushed, though Clare always managed somehow to see to it that her own staff managed to get something, if only a sandwich and a five-minute break.

She ate a ham salad, drank a cup of coffee and made her way back along the corridor, pausing at Reception to drop some letters given to her by patients into the post box. Through the glass swing doors she could see the ambulance still drawn up outside. The occupant had obviously been rushed through to Casualty and someone, no doubt a relative, was pacing the large, open reception area. Clare felt a quick stab of sympathy. The hospital was modern and very attractive. The designers had gone to endless trouble to make the surroundings pleasant for people who had to sit and wait. There were comfortable chairs, tables and magazines and masses of large plants, but it was still a hospital.

Clare's glance briefly took in the girl's appearance, though it was only a back view of long, elegant boots and a neatly tailored jacket and skirt. She was about to turn away but something held her, made her look again. It was only as her gaze reached the knot of pale, honey-blonde hair and the hands fumbling inexpertly with a cigarette that she felt the first stirrings of familiarity and with it a quick chill of alarm. She took a few steps in the girl's direction. It was something about the clothes, a certain style, chic, which put them somehow a little above the ordinary. She knew her reaction was totally illogical, but the colour was already draining from her face as her steps quickened and at that moment the girl turned.

Her mouth opened in a silent, anguished cry of recognition before she began to move and in the next instant had flung herself sobbing into Clare's arms.

'Clare, is it really you?' Her eyes seemed enormous in the whiteness of her distraught face, her accent, in the moment of stress, heavily defined.

'Danielle.' Only habit and training prevented Clare from giving way now to her own feelings of panic. Gently but firmly she led the weeping girl to a chair and sat beside her, listening to the frantic sobs, trying to interpret the French interspersed with heavily-accented English. 'What's happened. Why on earth are you here, at St Mary's of all places?'

'It is too terrible. There was an accident, Clare. It all happened so quickly, before I knew what was happening.' She pressed a shaking hand to her eyes. 'We had no chance. The car skidded. Oh, *mon Dieu*, I cannot believe it.' Tears oozed between her fingers. 'He is dead, I know he is dead. Why do they not tell me, let me go to him?'

Clare felt the iciness beginning to gather at the base of her spine. Gently she took the girl by the shoulders, shaking her. 'Who is dead, Danielle?' It took every effort of will not to give way to her own rising feelings of hysteria. It was as if a solid weight was suddenly being pressed down on her, but she had to ask the dreaded question. 'For pity's sake, Danielle, tell me.'

'Gray,' the reply stumbled out. 'He was driving.'

'Oh no, no.' Clare closed her eyes, willing herself not to faint. 'There must be some mistake.'

'I wish there were. Dear God, I wish it, but I came with him in the ambulance. He was not moving and he was so white.' Her hands wrung together helplessly. 'They won't let me see him, but why, unless he is dead?'

Clare swallowed hard and stood up. She felt a slight, but only very slight sense of relief, but her whole body was still shaking. 'That doesn't mean he is dead, Danielle, simply that they are still making an examination. It takes time.'

'But then why don't they let me see him or tell me . . . ?'

'I'm sure they will, just as soon as there is anything to tell. I know it seems needlessly cruel, but really it is for the best. The doctors can do their job more quickly and efficiently without the presence of the relatives.' She bit off the words, realising that, for all they were true, they were merely official words to this girl who needed comfort more. 'For Gray's sake it's best to let them do what they have to do.'

'I know.' Danielle sagged and began to weep again. 'But it is so hard.'

'Yes, it's always hard on the people who are waiting.' Clare found it difficult to speak. She found it impossible even to consider that Gray might be dead. How long had she loved him? Five, six years? It seemed like a lifetime. It hadn't been serious of course, merely an adolescent crush on a man who was so devastatingly handsome that the mere sight of him had been enough to take her breath away. She felt the colour flood into her cheeks. How glad she had been that he hadn't been aware of her childish adoration, hadn't even really thought of her as a person. Looking back on it later she saw the foolishness of it. She was simply Danielle's friend, a school friend whom Danielle had brought home to the château for a holiday because her parents were dead and no one wanted to spend the long summer vacation at school. And such holidays they had been, enjoyed with all the natural exuberance of fifteen years olds. The memories came back vividly, the dancing, the swimming, lying by the pool. It was there that she had first seen Gray Masterson, Danielle's guardian. She could almost laugh now, thinking how naive she must have been to think a man like Gray would notice a gawky, plain child whom he had seen for only minutes during each day of the long, hot summer which she had prayed would never end.

It had ended of course, and there had been one other, then no more. Her grandmother had died, she had sold the tiny cottage, taken possession of the few belongings which were in themselves a telling account of the simple, but happy life the old lady had led. There had been a little money, enough to enable Clare to find the flat where she now lived, and to begin her training at St Mary's. After that there had been no time to think of holidays. She had grown up, quickly, and Gray Masterson had become part of a past she had thought of occasionally, knowing it could never return, until now. But why, why had it had to happen like this, with such tragic irony?

She came out of her reverie with a start, realising that Danielle was speaking. 'I . . . I'm sorry?'

'I said you can find out what is happening? They will tell you.'

Clare frowned. 'It's not quite that easy. It's not as if I'm even working on Casualty.' With a cry of horror she looked at her watch. 'Oh, good heavens, I was supposed to be back on the ward ages ago.' She thought quickly, wishing she could avoid the silent look of helplessness in the other girl's face. 'Look, I'll contact my ward and get Staff to hold the fort. I must do that first. Then I'll see what I can do, but I can't make any promises.'

'But if you will try, it is all I ask.'

'I'll do my best. You sit here, I'll try and get you some coffee.'

'No, I do not want coffee, only to know that Gray is still alive.'

She was like a child, Clare thought, as she hurried away towards the nearest telephone. Sitting there with wisps of blonde hair against her pale cheeks. Danielle hadn't changed at all. She wondered if Gray had, after all he must be thirty now.

With Nightingale Ward in the competent hands of Staff Nurse O'Donnell Clare hurried back towards Casualty. It wasn't going to be easy to get any information. It wasn't as if she was a relative and her intrusion into the busy department wouldn't exactly be welcomed. It was with relief therefore that she saw the young registrar, Mike Davison, coming from the direction in which she was headed. Seeing her he stopped, hands in pockets, a look of obvious pleasure on his good-looking face.

'And to what do we owe this unexpected pleasure, Sister? Lost your way have you? Never mind, Uncle Mike'll take care of you. How about a coffee? I've got five minutes.' His arm slid round her shoulders with an easy affection which, at any other time, she would have enjoyed, even welcomed, but at the moment she found it impossible to respond and he sensed it.

'I came to enquire about a patient, Mike. He was admitted within the last quarter of an hour following a car accident. I wonder if you can tell me anything, his name is Masterson, Gray Masterson.'

The humour faded from his eyes as he saw the stricken look in her eyes.

'You know him?'

'Yes, he's a friend, at least . . .' her hand rose, 'his ward and I were at school together some years ago. She's waiting in Reception now and I promised to find out what I could. I realise I have no right . . .'

'Forget that.' He dismissed her protest lightly.

'It was sheer chance I happened to see her.' Clare felt the pulse hammering in her throat, realising that she was talking as a means of sheer escape. 'I said I'd try to find out what his condition is. Can you tell me anything, Mike, anything at all? Is he still alive?'

His hand was on her arm. 'Yes, he is.'

'Oh, thank God.' She released a breath faintly and his grip on her arm tightened.

'Look, where is this friend of yours? Let's go and find her then you can sit down and I can talk to you both.'

'Will you?' Her gaze jerked up gratefully and she allowed herself to be led back to where Danielle was pacing up and down the reception area. As she saw them she clasped a hand to her mouth. 'Gray, have you come to tell me . . . ?'

'No it isn't that.' Clare gave the quick reassurance. 'This is Mike Davison, a friend of mine. He's a registrar and has seen Gray.' She led Danielle to a group of red leather chairs set round a small low table and they all sat.

Mike hesitated. 'I'm afraid I can't tell you a great

deal. It's too soon to go into specific details, you realise that, don't you, Clare?'

She nodded. Danielle bit her lip.

'But he is still alive?'

'Yes, and a preliminary examination shows no severe internal injuries, though obviously we're waiting for the results of the X-rays and other tests and I'd rather we had them before giving you a more definite answer. He has a lacerated leg, it's pretty nasty but we can cope with that. Considerable bruising, but again that will heal fairly quickly.' He frowned and Clare looked up quickly.

'There's something else?'

He gave her an odd look. 'Well, we're not sure. It's going to take a little more time before we can be certain.' He looked at Danielle. 'I gather Mr Masterson hit his head during the accident?'

'Yes.' Her voice was little more than a whisper. She fumbled for a cigarette, putting it shakily to her lips. 'He was thrown forward against the windscreen.'

'Mm.'

'It is bad?'

Clare knew from watching his face that Mike Davison was worried. She didn't doubt that he was speaking the truth when he said it was too soon yet to be able to give a detailed picture of Gray's injuries, but she sensed that there was more to it than that. For some reason he was being deliberately evasive and felt uncomfortable because of it. He brushed a hand through his mop of curling brown hair, then, as if aware of her watching him, he looked up and his glance seemed to be appealing to her for something. Bleakly she understood. He was asking her to help him keep his real concern from Danielle.

She spoke briskly. 'How long before you get the results of all the tests?'

'A couple of days before we have them all, and then we may need to do some more.'

Danielle looked quickly from Clare to Mike. 'But you haven't said what is wrong with Gray. You asked if he had hit his head.'

'Yes, well that was strictly routine. He has a severe concussion and we always like to know the precise cause of the injury if possible. It helps.' He smiled and it was the kind of smile Clare had seen before. It helped to reassure and Danielle reacted to it now.

She nodded. 'What is going to happen to him now?'

'He'll be admitted, of course, and as soon as the preliminary examinations are completed he'll be sent up to the ward. Yours I imagine, Sister. You do have a bed?'

'A side ward. We're pretty full. I checked just before I came down.' Her voice trailed away. It was a bitter irony that Gray was actually being admitted to her ward, yet she felt relieved. If he had to be anywhere she was glad it was where she would be able to see him constantly. 'As a matter of fact I'd better get back there now. Staff will want to know what's happening.' She tried to speak calmly despite the fact that her heart was hammering beneath the navy uniform. 'Danielle, will you wait here? You'll find a vending machine over there, and magazines. I'll get back to you as soon as I can, I promise.'

'I'll be all right.'

'Try not to worry. We'll sort something out and Gray will be fine, won't he, Mike?'

'He couldn't be in better hands.' Mike grinned, but as they moved away together Clare looked at him anxiously.

'What's wrong, Mike? I know there's something. I can understand that you don't want to worry Danielle, but I'm not the panicking sort, not really,' she laughed wryly. 'I'd rather know.'

He paused as they came to the swing doors. 'I honestly can't tell you much. There is something,' he frowned. 'It's difficult to be sure. That head injury complicated things, there's some damage to his eyes but . . . it's not that so much that's giving us the trouble.' His mouth compressed for a moment. 'It may be nothing, but Westlake has been sent for. He'll be seeing him tomorrow.'

Clare felt her whole body go rigid. 'Westlake? But . . . he's a neurologist.'

'That's right.'

'But . . . I don't understand. You said Gray has concussion.'

'Yes, he has.' Suddenly he was avoiding her gaze. 'Look, honestly Clare, that's as much as I know at the moment. I've got to get back but I promise, as soon as I know any more I'll tell you.'

She stood watching as he hurried away and began

to make her own way back to the ward. In two hours she was due to go off duty but she knew that nothing would induce her to leave until she knew what was wrong with Gray.

She stood outside the ward, shivering, feeling suddenly cold and very vulnerable. Ever since she was a child she had dreamed of becoming a nurse, but she hadn't realised then that she would ever become personally involved. Now she was. Not that Gray Masterson still meant anything to her of course. But all the same, for the first time, tragedy seemed to have struck too close to home and she didn't know how she was going to get through the next hours or days or weeks.

CHAPTER TWO

CLARE sat at the desk, forcing herself to behave calmly. Habit died hard and for once she was glad of it. The night report had to be written up before the day staff came on duty. Her hand shook. Gray's name had never been part of it before.

The lift doors whirred softly in the corridor outside the ward. Taking a deep breath she went forward to meet the trolley which was being pushed by two porters. She held the swing doors open as they manoeuvred it through, careful not to dislodge the intravenous drip. Clare moved automatically to hold it and as she did so her heart lurched as she looked down at the still figure.

Gray's eyes were closed, his face was ashen. It was as much as she had time to notice, but the strength of her recognition was so intense that she felt a sudden chill run through her. The five years might have been no more than five minutes. He was just as she remembered him. She had steeled herself to find him changed, but the knowledge that her memory had distorted nothing made the sight of him all the harder to bear.

Her movements were purely automatic as he was wheeled into the side ward and lifted on to the bed. He groaned slightly. Her hand reached out and his fingers closed tightly over it.

'Don't worry, you're going to be fine. We're just

going to get you into bed and make you comfortable, then you can go to sleep.'

Just for an instant the hand holding hers seemed to relax and she had to shake off the crazy idea that he had actually recognised her voice. It wasn't possible. He was a patient in pain and glad of any human contact, but for some reason the disappointment stayed with her even after the porters had gone and she moved about the small room, filling in the fresh chart which was clipped at the foot of the bed. Returning it to its place she stood for a moment and her breath caught in her throat as the light from the shaded lamp above the bed was reflected onto his face. It was gaunt, shadowed by pain, making him seem strangely vulnerable, almost like a child. Beneath the sandy brown hair his eyes were closed, but she knew that when he opened them they would be brown. Five years ago she had looked up at him and smiled. He had smiled back, briefly, and she, a child, not yet a woman but with all the awakening instincts of one, had known she loved him just as she knew now that nothing was changed. The bitter irony of it was that Gray probably wouldn't even remember her name.

She crossed to the window, edging aside the curtains to stare out into the artificial light cast onto the hospital drive below. An eerie stillness seemed to have settled over everything. It wasn't just the fine covering of snow, it was something which she and every nurse and patient came to recognise, the uneasy hour when pain was at its greatest and fears always seemed worse.

Letting the curtain fall she shook herself mentally and moved quietly to the bedside. What was wrong with her? She, of all people, ought to know better than to give way to those fears. Gray was going to get better. 'Please, please get better, for my sake.' She wasn't even aware that she had whispered the words aloud until Kathy O'Donnell spoke, quietly, from the open doorway.

'I'm sorry, Sister, did you say something?'

'What . . . oh no, just checking the notes and thinking aloud. It's a bad habit.' Briskly, a little embarrassed, she checked the drip, added a note to the clip-board and put her pen away.

The other girl's gaze sought Clare's, full of sympathy. 'I'm sure he'll be all right, Sister.'

'Yes, I'm sure he will, too, Staff.' Clare nodded, moving unsteadily to the door where she paused. 'He's down to see Mr Westlake tomorrow afternoon.'

'That's right, Sister. But I doubt if there will be any more definite news for a few days.'

Back in the office, Clare bent her head purposefully over her notes. The report completed at last she sat back, her fingers drumming quietly against the book, then she glanced at her watch. Tiredness was beginning to catch up. 'I'd better go and see Miss Neuville and explain what's happening or, at least, as much as I can.'

'I sent one of the students down a while ago, to make sure she had some coffee,' Kathy said. 'Poor girl, she looks badly shaken up.'

'Yes, it's been quite a shock, I'm sure. Come to

think of it, I don't even know where she is staying.'
Clare's brow furrowed. 'I may have to make some
arrangements.' She was still frowning as she made
her way briskly down to Reception again.

Danielle was sitting hunched on a chair, a plastic
beaker of coffee abandoned on the low table in
front of her, a cigarette in her hand. She stubbed it
out, her eyes widening anxiously in the soft oval of
her face as Clare approached.

'What is happening? Is Gray going to be all right?
Why won't they let me see him?'

Clare gently urged the girl to sit again. 'He's not
long been settled in the ward and at the moment
he's sleeping. We want him to get as much rest as
possible, but by tomorrow you'll be able to come
and see him.' She laughed dully. 'I mean later
today. I always seem to lose track of time when I'm
on night duty.' She knew she was purposely avoiding telling Danielle that everything was going to be
fine, when as yet so many questions still remained
unanswered. 'He's quite comfortable.' The words
sounded trite, even to her own ears. They were the
standard reassurance, perfectly legitimate but
Danielle wasn't fooled. She looked at Clare, helpless uncertainty in her eyes.

'But what does that mean? When will he be able
to go home?'

'Well, not just yet. He had a pretty nasty bang on
the head, you know, and his leg is broken. It's going
to take a little time.'

'How much time?'

'I'm—not really sure yet, but I should think by

tomorrow we'll have more news.' Clare hesitated. 'Mr Westlake is due to see him.'

'Westlake? Yes, your friend mentioned him, but why? The doctor has already seen Gray.'

'Yes, I know, but Mr Westlake is a neurologist.' She saw the flicker of fear in the girl's eyes. 'He specialises in problems connected with the nervous system.'

'I know what it means, but I don't understand why. Gray had an accident.' There were tears in the blue eyes now, a hint of exhaustion in her voice which made Clare put an arm about her shoulders.

'Try not to worry. Gray is getting the best possible care.'

'Then why does he have to see this man . . . Westlake?'

'It isn't all that unusual really.' Clare hated the false brightness she heard in her own voice, but in a way it was for her own reassurance as much as for Danielle's. She glanced at her watch. 'Look, it's late, or early, whichever way you want to look at it. I'm going off duty soon. Where were you and Gray staying?'

Danielle brushed a hand across her eyes. 'An hotel. Gray arranged it.'

'Can you remember which one?'

Danielle gave her the name of an exclusive hotel not too far from the hospital. Clare recognised it as one she passed every day as she drove to work. 'I know it.'

'We were to stay there for another two days before going back to France.' Her voice trailed away on a sob. 'It was my fault. We should have returned a week ago but I was enjoying myself so much.' Her eyes lifted bleakly to Clare. 'If I hadn't persuaded him . . .'

'That's nonsense,' Clare managed, through tight lips. 'You're upset, probably in a state of shock, but no-one could possibly have known this would happen. You can't take the blame on yourself. It was a chance in a million.' *And it had to happen to Gray*. The thought hammered in her brain and she had to draw herself up sharply. She was falling into the trap herself, letting tiredness and tension affect her judgment. 'You need some sleep.' For the first time she noticed the spots of blood on Danielle's beautifully cut skirt and felt a tremor run through her. She got to her feet. 'Shall I see you back to your hotel or would you rather come home with me? I have a flat. It's within easy reach of the hospital. It's small, I'm afraid, but I do have a spare bed.'

'Would you mind.' Relief brought a little of the colour back to the girl's cheeks. 'I don't think I could bear to be alone, not now.'

'Of course I don't mind. Anyway,' she smiled, 'we have a lot of catching up to do. Five years of it. It's been a long time. So much has happened.' For an incredible moment her heart lurched. She didn't even know if Gray was married. 'Is . . . is there anyone else who should be notified?' Her mouth was dry, but Danielle shook her head.

'No. No-one.'

She felt almost ashamed of the surge of relief which flooded through her. 'I'll get in touch with the hotel and explain the situation. We can arrange to settle the bill and have your things moved tomorrow, when the picture is a little clearer.'

Danielle gathered up her bag and got to her feet, frowning. 'Actually, yes, there is someone I should contact. I must ring Alain.'

'Alain?'

'Alain Duval. Gray's doctor. He will want to know what has happened. 'We've all been friends for many years. He will know what to do.'

'But, isn't it a little soon? I mean, there's very little you can actually tell at the moment and it's not as if he'll be able to do anything, not while Gray is here.'

'I know that,' Danielle's brow puckered impatiently. 'But I don't intend that Gray shall remain here.'

Clare felt an odd sinking feeling in the pit of her stomach. 'What do you mean?'

'Why, I shall take him home, of course. What else?'

Clare could hardly speak. 'But that may be dangerous. He couldn't possibly be moved yet, certainly not until the results of the tests are known and even then it may be some time.'

Danielle's hand dismissed the arguments. 'I shall speak to Alain. He will know what is best. I told you, we are friends.'

And I am not, Clare thought, dully, managing somehow to bite back the response. The stubborn look on the other girl's face was something she had forgotten until now, but it was something she had seen often enough in the past and knew that no amount of arguing would persuade Danielle to change her mind. Just for a moment she almost hated this Alain Duval, then dismissed the idea as ridiculous. After all, she had never met him and he was a doctor, his main concern would be for the welfare of any patient. Surely he would be able to make Danielle see that her idea was unwise.

Weariness was suddenly catching up; she felt drained and cold. It was probably the result of shock as much as mere physical tiredness, but all she wanted at this moment was to get home. Arguments and reasoning could wait.

'Shall we go?' She hunted in her bag for the keys of her Mini and Danielle nodded, mutely. Her mouth drooped miserably. 'I wish I'd never asked Gray to bring me to England.'

Clare couldn't answer. How could she say that she almost wished it too. That she would rather have been spared the torment of seeing Gray again under circumstances like these, especially if she was to lose him again so soon if Danielle had her way.

She slept fitfully for a few hours. By late afternoon when she got up the overnight snow had almost vanished and the roads were completely clear as she drove back on duty. She had seen Danielle only briefly as she had returned from the hospital after visiting Gray. Her expression was troubled and tinged with annoyance as she threw her bag and fur coat onto a chair.

Clare, making coffee before she had to leave, was already dressed in her uniform. In spite of her tiredness she hadn't been able to sleep deeply either. The temptation to get out of bed and go and visit Gray had been strong but she had fought it, knowing that she wasn't going to be of any use at all on duty, either to herself or to Gray, if she was too exhausted to do her job properly. And anyway, it wasn't as if she was a relative. She had no special privileges.

When finally she had got up and automatically made herself a snack to eat, Danielle's note had been propped against the kettle. Reading it, Clare had had to force down a feeling of resentment that Danielle could see him whenever she pleased. Knowing that the thought was uncharitable didn't make it hurt any the less. And now Danielle was back, her face sullen as she dropped wearily into a chair.

'They wouldn't let me see him for more than a few minutes. What right have they to keep me away.' Red fingernails drummed angrily against the chair and Clare felt her own fingers tighten round the handle of the coffee pot.

'Is Gray any worse? Surely they would have phoned.'

'No, there is no change. At least, they say there is not, but he is so pale, just lying there.'

Clare felt her heart contract painfully. For one awful moment she imagined something must have happened, that Gray's condition must have de-

teriorated. Now, relief surged through her like a
wave.

'I should have warned you that you probably
wouldn't be allowed to see him for more than a few
minutes.' She poured two cups of coffee. Danielle
took hers, ungraciously refusing sugar. 'It's quite
normal procedure after an accident, especially
when the patient is in shock. In any case, Gray was
due to see Mr Westlake today. It's possible the tests
may have tired him.'

'But they wouldn't tell me the results of the
tests.'

'No.' Clare stifled a pang of impatience at the
girl's manner. 'But that's not because they didn't
want you to know. It's simply that there would be
nothing to tell as yet. Believe me, as soon as they
know anything you will be told.'

'Oh, it's so easy for you to say that, to take it all so
calmly. You're a nurse. These things mean nothing
to you.'

Clare had to remind herself that it was fear
rousing Danielle's volatile temper, but she felt her
own face whitening. She set her cup down, spilling
some of the contents. 'That isn't exactly true. Yes, I
am a nurse. I condition myself not to become
over-emotional, but that doesn't mean I don't care.
As a matter of fact . . . I'm very fond of Gray too.'
She swallowed hard. 'I'm as anxious as you are that
he should get well again.'

Danielle's gaze studied her for a moment, then
flickered. 'Yes, of course you are. Forgive me. I
forget you knew Gray, but it was a long time ago.

We were children. I didn't think you would remember.'

Her voice was stiff, unnatural. Clare watched as the slender fingers fumbled for a cigarette. In a way she felt sorry for Danielle. She had always taken so many things for granted.

'Those summer holidays I spent at the château were very special to me. I have every reason to be grateful to Gray for allowing them to happen.' Suddenly the coffee tasted bitter and she got to her feet quickly, putting on her navy uniform coat and buttoning it. 'I have to go on duty. Will you be all right.'

'But of course.' Danielle rose with unconscious grace and crossed to the window. She didn't turn as she spoke. 'By the way, I telephoned Alain this morning.'

At the door Clare froze in her tracks. The mere mention of that man's name was enough to set her heart hammering. 'And?'

Danielle's shoulders were lifted in a shrug. 'He agrees with me. As soon as it is possible, Gray should return home.'

Shock held Clare rigid. 'You realise it may still be some time? I did try to warn you last night . . .'

'I know. But you are not the doctor, are you, Clare?' Danielle turned at last and Clare was shocked by the tautness of the beautiful features.

'No, I'm not a doctor,' she said, quietly, 'but I've seen a lot of cases like this and I know that miracles don't happen overnight. All I'm saying is be patient.'

'That isn't so easy.' The dark eyes seemed suddenly larger in the girl's stricken face. 'Gray means so much to me. He is all I have. He has been father, mother, brother to me. If anything were to happen . . .' Her voice broke on a sob. 'You see why I had to speak to Alain.'

'Yes, of course I do. It's just that I don't see what he can do.'

'Well, we don't know do we?' Danielle's voice rose, sharply. 'That is why he is coming over. He was going to book a flight the moment he had finished talking to me.'

Clare felt as if she had been hit by a blast of cold air. Just who did this . . . Alain Duval think he was. 'I see.'

'Wait. Clare please.' Danielle's voice halted her as she turned blindly to the door.

'I shall be late. I should have left ten minutes ago.'

'I know and I'm sorry. Clare, I've been thinking, whenever it happens, sooner or later, Gray is going to need nursing. He will resent it of course. Gray isn't the sort of person to take kindly to having his movements restricted, he's too fond of a good time for that.' Her laughter faded uneasily into a long silence. 'I . . . I know I have no right to ask it, but when it is possible to take him home to France, will you come with us, to look after him?'

Clare stared at her in stunned silence. Her head was reeling. 'Are you serious? Why me?'

'Why not?' Danielle was looking at her directly. 'You know him. You know the château. He would accept better someone who was not a complete stranger.'

'Has it occurred to you that he may not even remember me? You said yourself, it was a long time ago.'

'He will.' Danielle moved closer, her eyes appealing. 'I think he may already have done so. Today, when I was with him, he spoke your name.'

Incredulity robbed Clare momentarily of speech. 'But . . . you must have been mistaken.'

'No, he said it quite clearly.'

It wasn't possible. It couldn't be yet, for those few brief seconds when she had held his hand, offering reassurance, his fingers had tightened. Her voice shook. 'Even if he remembers me, aren't you rather assuming the worst? Gray may not need a nurse. In any case your Dr Duval may have ideas of his own about that.' And most likely would, she thought, with rare irritation. She knew next to nothing about the man, yet for some reason the mere mention of his name set her teeth on edge and the very thought of having to work closely with someone so arrogant that he could presume to know what was best for Gray without having even seen him . . .

'*I* am asking you, Clare, as my friend. We've known each other for a long time. I don't want strangers around Gray and he is going to need you.' Her voice faltered and Clare was shocked to see the tears suddenly coursing onto her cheeks. 'Clare, he is blind.'

Horror froze Clare's voice in her throat. She

shook her head, not wanting to believe. 'There must be some mistake. It can't be true, not Gray.'

'But it is. He looked at me, straight at me, and he didn't see me.' Danielle covered her face with her hands. 'Have you any idea what that will mean to Gray of all people? He won't be able to paint. His career will be over almost before it has begun. *Mon Dieu*, how could it happen? Why Gray? It should have been me.' She was sobbing distractedly now. Clare went to her without even being aware of what she did, putting her arms around her.

'It may not be as bad as you think. The damage may be temporary, it does happen.' She knew that she was trying to reassure herself as much as the other girl, and she wasn't succeeding. 'Did you speak to anyone about it?'

'But of course. I saw your friend, Dr Davison.'

'And what did he say?'

'What could he say? He told me they are still waiting, always waiting. That they couldn't say yet whether Gray will be blind or not.' Her hands clenched together. 'I can't bear it. I wish Alain were here, he would know what to do.'

Clare bit back an angry response. In any case she was more concerned with Mike Davison's comment. She trusted his judgment and suddenly the need to talk to him, to find out the truth, as much as it was possible to discover at this stage, was overwhelming. 'Look, Danielle, I have to go on duty.' Gently she released the girl, but Danielle held her back.

'But say you will come with us to France, please.'

'I'll have to think about it. It isn't quite that simple and, as I said, it may not even be necessary.'

Danielle released her, her face suddenly rigid. 'Whatever happens, I mean to take Gray home, Clare. If you come it will be easier. So consider, for his sake. If he has to face the worst it may be easier coming from you than a complete stranger.'

Clare stared at her. She wanted to say, 'You don't know what you are asking. Why me?' But the words wouldn't come. She opened the door. 'Try to get some rest. If anything happens I'll call you, I promise.'

She was scarcely aware of driving to the hospital or of making her way up to the ward. Luckily everything was quiet. The bad weather seemed to have kept people at home, off the roads. Even Casualty had been quiet as she had come by. The lull before the storm perhaps. It went like that, in spasms.

Having taken over the ward officially she went quietly into the sideward almost dreading what she might find. The shaded lamp cast shadows onto the pale face against the pillows and a sudden chill gripped at her heart. Gray's eyes were closed, she wanted to smooth the hair away from his face, hair which wasn't quite as dark as she remembered. There was something almost boyish about his features, a hint of plumpness. Perhaps he had changed, just a little, but looks were only basic. He was still the same Gray Masterson and she loved him.

It was some seconds before she realised that his

eyes were open and he was staring up at her. She caught her breath, feeling a tiny tremor of shock. Danielle had been wrong. Gray could see. It had all been some ghastly mistake.

He turned his head against the pillow. 'Is someone there? Damn these eyes of mine. I know there is, I can hear you breathing. Why don't you say something?'

She felt the colour drain from her face and was glad he couldn't see the tears sparkling in her eyes. Her throat was dry, aching with compassion as she forced herself to speak.

'Hullo. I'm sorry, did I wake you?'

'No, at least I don't think so.' His hand went, restlessly, to his eyes. 'It's this infernal headache. Can't seem to shift it.'

She took the chart from the end of his bed, studying the prescribed medication. 'You're due for some more tablets soon. They should help. I'm afraid it was quite a nasty bang on the head you had. But it should be better in a few days.'

'A few days. They can seem like a lifetime when you're just lying here.'

She was surprised by the note of bitterness in his tone. For a moment he had sounded just like a child deprived of its favourite toy. Then she reminded herself that he was in pain and probably still suffering from shock. 'I know.' Her lips formed a smile even as she remembered that he couldn't see the gesture. 'But it won't be for too long.'

His lips twisted, disbelievingly. 'That's what they keep saying, but no one has actually told me yet why I can't see properly.'

She had to stop herself from over-reacting. 'You mean . . . you can see something?'

'Shadows, sometimes.' His hand tightened against the covers. 'Am I going to be able to see again?' He reached out and involuntarily she put her hand into his, feeling his fingers tighten as they had before.

'I haven't spoken to the doctor. I only came on duty a short time ago so I really don't know what results they have had yet from the tests which have been done so far. But you mustn't expect the worst.'

He laughed, bitterly. 'My God, how easily everyone says that. What the hell do they know about it, or me? I'm an artist, or at least I was. What sort will I be without the use of my eyes?'

'I know. And you're a very good one.' She said it quietly, without thinking and saw the frown etch its way into his brow.

'You know? Well, well. I wouldn't have thought the word had gone around already. It's not as if I've exactly made a name for myself yet.'

'Maybe not, but you will. You must learn to have a little faith in yourself, and the doctors. They are doing their best, you know.'

There was something about the way he seemed to stare at her which made her feel uneasy, almost as if he could see the changing expressions on her face which she was trying so hard to hide. Something was obviously troubling him.

'I know you, don't I? We've met before?' His

other hand rose to probe a nerve in his temple as if it could clear his memory. 'You spoke to me when I was brought up to the ward.'

'Yes, that's right.'

'But it's not just that, there's something about you, your voice.'

Her heart thudded. 'Don't worry about it. It's not important. You should try to get some rest.'

'But it is important, to me.' The pressure of his hand tightened on her own. 'It's funny, I've heard people say that when your sight goes your other senses become more acute. I just hadn't realised it would happen so quickly.'

'I don't think it has.' She found it difficult to speak. 'You were a bit dozy when they brought you up here and I happened to be around. I spoke to you and you remembered my voice.' She didn't want to believe that was all it was. Disappointment brought the tears welling up and she couldn't brush them away because he held her hand.

'I know the memory can play tricks, but tell me your name, please. I don't think it was just yesterday. We've met before, I'm sure of it. Put me out of my misery.'

She laughed unsteadily. 'Yes, we have, but it was a long time ago, you couldn't possibly remember.'

'If you're trying to tell me I'm still in a state of shock, you may be right, but my mind is perfectly clear at this moment.' He frowned. 'It's . . . Clare. Clare . . . ?'

'Summers.' Her voice sounded strangely unlike her own. 'Danielle and I were at school together.

She invited me to spend a couple of holidays with her at the château. You were there, of course, but you couldn't possibly remember a mere schoolgirl, especially one as awkward and plain as I was.'

There was a long silence and she felt a momentary pang of alarm. What was she thinking of, to let him over-tax himself so soon after the accident? 'Don't worry, you're bound to be a bit hazy, especially about things that happened several years ago. Amnesia isn't at all uncommon after a head injury. I shouldn't have let you talk. It's not important.'

'But you're wrong.' He said it very quietly. 'I do remember, quite clearly as a matter of fact, and you do yourself an injustice. You were never awkward, or plain. Shy perhaps. I seem to recall that every time I came in sight you blushed and hid yourself away somewhere. I wondered why? Was I really such an ogre, Clare?'

He was teasing, she knew it, but it was a gentle teasing and her heart was behaving crazily. 'I . . . I suppose I was shy, but more than anything I knew you couldn't possibly appreciate having an unwanted schoolgirl thrust upon you for the holidays.'

'My dear girl,' his hand was drawing her relentlessly towards him now, 'You were never unwanted. On the contrary,' his fingers were stroking her hand, 'Danielle's friends were always welcome and still are, but you never gave me the chance to get to know you.' He frowned again. 'How old are you now? Eighteen, nineteen?'

She laughed, breathlessly. 'Twenty-two.'

'Twenty-two?' His brow rose. 'And not a child

any longer.' Then his face clouded. 'Fate can be bloody unfair. I'd like to see if you turned out to be as beautiful as I was always sure you would. I seem to remember those long legs of yours. You reminded me of a young filly, running around the swimming pool.'

Her voice shook. 'I'm not beautiful.'

'Oh come now, Nurse, aren't you being a little too modest?' The voice coming so unexpectedly from behind her sent her spinning round to look at the stranger standing there. The thought that he had been eavesdropping, particularly on a conversation which was so very private, sent a blaze of colour flooding into her cheeks as she stared at the lean, handsome face which was studying her with such open disapproval now. Even through her anger she was aware of the aquiline nose and firm, stubborn jaw. The fact that he regarded her with such sardonic amusement made her free her hand from Gray's grasp. The movement was imperceptible but she was well aware that he had noticed it. Indeed, she had the feeling that very little escaped those piercingly blue eyes which raked her from head to toe with such disturbing arrogance, as if she was a piece of merchandise.

Her chin rose, defiantly. How dare he presume to judge her? She didn't even know the man and what was he doing here on the ward anyway? Her lips parted to ask the questions, but it was Gray who, unknowingly, supplied the answers and she felt her heart sink in dismay.

'Alain? Alain, is that you?' The note of incredulity and pleasure in his voice made her throat tighten.

Oh no, it couldn't be. Almost as if he was aware of her hostility, the keen eyes narrowed and she had the feeling that he was mocking her.

'That's right. Sorry I couldn't get here any sooner, old man, though perhaps it's just as well. I have the distinct feeling I intruded at precisely the wrong moment.'

She felt herself go hot at the edge of cynicism in his voice. She determined not to let it reach her, but there was something distinctly un-nerving about that cool glance. It was as if he had reduced her to the state of a young junior, caught in a misdeed by her superior. Except that she was not guilty of any crime and he was certainly not her superior.

'May I ask just what you are doing here?' Her voice sounded sharp, uneven. Annoyingly he had also apparently the ability to rob her of her usual calm and poise. In an attempt to regain it she drew herself up, smoothing the skirts of her navy dress and glancing at her watch. 'I'm afraid visiting hours ended at eight o'clock and we have very strict regulations.'

'I'm sure you do, Nurse, though it seems you don't apply them all quite so rigidly.'

She gasped at what was so obviously a reference to the fact that she had been holding Gray's hand. A denial rose to her lips. It hadn't been like that. He didn't know the circumstances and he had no right to judge. But Gray, apparently unaware of the tension, intervened.

'Clare, my sweet, this isn't any ordinary visitor, this is a good friend of mine, from France, though God knows how he knew, or got here so quickly. This is Alain, Alain Duval. Oh damn these eyes of mine, I wish I could see. Where are you?'

'Don't worry about it, Gray, my friend. I'm here.' She watched, helplessly, as, ignoring her presence, he moved towards the bed and clasped Gray's hand, shaking it firmly. He had large hands she noticed, then shifted her gaze as the blue eyes swept momentarily over her again. For a moment she was puzzled. They contained almost a hint of . . . warning, or was it a plea? 'Danielle called me and said you'd had a bit of an accident. I was coming over anyway so I thought I'd combine business with pleasure.' He was smiling and Clare was made crazily aware of a mouth which in repose was gentle, sensuous, yet there was a suggestion of cruelty and arrogance about it too, emotions which, she guessed, would be easily aroused in this man, and she wouldn't care to be on the receiving end if it were ever the case.

'How are you feeling now?'

Gray shrugged. 'I'm fine. It's just these eyes of mine, playing tricks. And of course no-one tells me anything.'

Clare was immediately on the defensive. 'I've explained to you, Gray, that the tests take time.'

'Tests! That's all very well, but I'm the one who has to lie here. I'm beginning to wonder if this guy, Westlake, really knows what he's doing.'

'I think that's a little unfair, Gray.' She felt the

spots of colour in her cheeks deepen and murmured
a sharp protest as Alain Duval calmly walked to the
end of the bed, removed the clip board and began
studying the confidential notes.

Her hand was flung out to remove them from his
grasp. 'Look, you can't do that. Please put them
back, this instant.'

To her chagrin her protest was ignored. 'I'm
quite capable of returning it to its proper place
when I'm ready, Nurse.' She could only watch,
helplessly, as he held it beyond her reach, then he
looked at Gray. 'Nurse is right, my friend, and you
always were impatient as the devil.'

The sullen look was there again on Gray's face. 'I
think you would be too, in my place.'

The sensuous mouth actually smiled. 'Yes, I
suppose I would.' The chart was returned to its clip.
Angrily, and unnecessarily, Clare straightened it
and faced the stranger, breathing hard.

'Monsieur . . .'

'Doctor.'

She gritted her teeth. 'I am well aware of the fact,
Doctor. Danielle did tell me a little about you.'

The dark brow rose. 'Good for Danielle. Can
you pass me the ophthalmoscope Nurse?'

Her breath was released in a rush of fury. 'Sister.
And no, I can't. Doctor, how dare you? Must I
remind you that you have absolutely no jurisdiction
here. You can't simply walk into this hospital and
take over. Will you please leave now, or must I ring
for assistance and have you removed?'

The dark gaze stared with maddening calm down

into hers. 'By all means, do so if you wish, Sister, I cannot prevent you, but I think you may find you will look a little foolish.' She saw the pulse beating in his throat as he took the ophthalmoscope from her numbed fingers. 'Now, Gray, let me just take a quick look at these eyes of yours.'

Disbelieving, she watched open mouthed as he proceeded to make the examination. After some moments he straightened up and there was a grim set to his mouth which momentarily clouded the handsome features, yet his voice when he spoke, was quite calm. 'Well that must have been quite some knock you took.'

'Yes, I suppose it was.' Gray agreed, dully. 'But what about my eyes?'

For one instant Clare's gaze flew beseechingly to the tall figure. He met it expressionlessly, but there was surprising gentleness in his voice.

'Now surely you don't imagine I could tell you anything from so brief an examination, my friend, and it would be unfair to speculate. But I will do more tests, that I promise, and I'll have you back on your feet in no time.

Clare had to clench her hands to stop them shaking. She couldn't believe what was happening. 'You have no right to make such promises.' Her voice lowered so that Gray wouldn't hear. 'And as for making more tests, that will not be possible or necessary . . .'

'Oh but I disagree. It is both possible and necessary, but have no fear, Sister, I have no intention of abusing the facilities of your beloved ward.'

'Wh . . . what do you mean?'

His voice was cold as he studied her. 'It's quite simple, I have made arrangements to have Mr Masterson taken home to France. I shall escort him personally of course.'

Her face was white as she stared up at him. 'But that is out of the question. He can't possibly be moved.'

'I regret that you have so little faith, Sister, but I assure you it is quite possible, in fact we shall be leaving within the week.'

Clare felt cold and sick. 'And I regret that you may be forced to alter your plans. Mr Westlake will almost certainly wish to make further tests himself and I don't imagine he will take kindly to your interference.'

The dark eyes were hard and unsmiling. 'Whatever you may imagine, I am not so lacking in either ethics or courtesy that I would presume to . . . interfere, as you put it. I am fully aquainted with Mr Westlake's intentions.'

She felt her cheeks blazing with colour. 'That wasn't the impression I was given, Doctor.'

The sensuous mouth contorted, mockingly. 'Impressions are not always reliable, Sister, as you yourself must be well aware. However, it may reassure you to know that I spent an hour in consultation with Mr Westlake this afternoon. In fact he and I are old colleagues. I had the privilege of training under him several years ago.' The knowledge surprised her but she had no intention of allowing him to see it. She was unprepared how-

ever for the hand which closed tightly over her arm
as he propelled her away from the bed, ignoring her
protests. His voice was lowered, threatening and
the contact sent a sudden shock running through
her. He was strong and brutal and she knew that,
were she to make a real enemy of him, he would
show no mercy. 'Gray will come to no more harm
for being moved, provided the necessary precau-
tions are taken, and they will be. The truth is,
Sister, that it may be better to make the journey
now than later. Surely you must have guessed that
there is a good possibility he will become completely blind in time, unless we can do something to save
his sight.'

'Are you saying it is possible?' She whispered.

He shook his head. 'I don't know. I don't make
idle promises, but I'm sure if you think about it,
you'll see the wisdom of what I'm doing and that it
matters more than some . . . idle flirtation with a
patient.'

She flinched. 'It wasn't what you thought.'

'Frankly, I don't care what it was. In any case,
this doesn't really concern you. I mean to take my
patient back to France where I can see to it that
there are no distractions and he can concentrate
simply on the treatment I shall devise for him. Is
that clear, Sister?'

With as much dignity as she could muster she
wrenched her arm free of his grasp. She was breathing hard and felt the tears threatening. 'My only
concern is that Gray should get better, Doctor,
nothing else matters.'

'Then we're agreed on that at least. Now I suggest you leave the patient to sleep. He's going to need all the rest he can get during the next few days.'

Stunned she managed, somehow, to walk past him and return to the office where she sank into the chair and rested her head in her hands. The shock that Gray might lose his sight permanently was still too much to take in. The fact that he would be at the tender mercies of a man like Alain Duval was too much to bear. He was completely inhuman and what Gray needed was love and understanding if he was ever to come to terms with his blindness and face the future. She sat up, staring at the clock in front of her. The future. She could make it possible for Gray, if he would let her. She could be his eyes, she would love him, protect him.

Slowly she picked up the phone and dialled the number of her flat. Danielle answered.

'Hullo, Danielle. I've been thinking about what you said. I will come with you to France. You were right, I think Gray may need me.' She put the receiver down and realised her hands were shaking. Alain Duval wasn't going to like it, but that was a bridge she would cross when she came to it. For the moment Gray was the only thing that mattered and nothing and no-one was going to stop her being with him.

CHAPTER THREE

THEY could scarcely have had a better day for the crossing to France. No doubt Alain Duval had taken care of that too, Clare thought, irritably, as she moved about the comfortable cabin, checking that her patient was quite comfortable. He had managed everything else with an arrogance which, she was beginning to realise, was so typical of him, before taking a flight back to France himself. No doubt confident in the thought that even the weather wouldn't dare to disobey his instructions. To her chagrin, Clare had to admit that certainly he had succeeded because nothing had gone wrong and she was only glad that she didn't have to see the confident look in those devastating eyes. It had been quite bad enough having him stand in her office, its small confines suddenly made to seem claustrophobic by his presence, Dr Westlake beside him, the two of them discussing Gray as if they were old friends. What was even more surprising was the apparent calm with which the normally irascible consultant had accepted, even approved, the abrupt removal of one of his patients from his care. Clare had found herself standing dumbstruck and angry as they discussed it, almost as if she weren't even present. Only when James Westlake had finally bustled away did Alain Duval look up from the

50

notes he was writing, his face grim, a frown of impatience furrowing his brow.

He's not even really seeing me, Clare thought. I'm just a body in a uniform. I could be a little first-year student for all he cares. Yet she had the uneasy feeling that even had she been the Divisional Nursing Officer Alain Duval would still have got his own way.

'I've taken care of all the arrangements.' His voice had brought her sharply out of her reverie and she had found herself standing, hands clasped in front of her just as if she were being reprimanded. Her mouth tightened, blast the man. 'Unfortunately I have to catch the first flight back to France myself.' The thought brought the only glimmer of relief as she found herself unconsciously studying his face and she was surprised to note the faint lines of weariness etched there.

'You're going back tonight? But you haven't had any rest.'

'I'll survive. I'm taking the first flight. Tonight if possible, tomorrow morning at the latest. It rather depends on how long it takes to get things sorted out here, Sister.'

She felt herself colour faintly at the obvious rebuke, as if she had been keeping him unnecessarily. 'I assure you, you can count on me to do everything possible to speed you on your way, Doctor.' Her voice was purposely demure and she had the satisfaction of seeing the momentary flicker of doubt cross his handsome features before he looked away from her serious face.

'I'm quite sure I can, Sister. It shouldn't take up too much of your valuable time and I can snatch half an hour's sleep on the plane. My car will be at the airport to meet me so I can doze again then. I'm used to it. In any case, I don't need much sleep and my one concern at the moment is to get my patient settled as quickly as possible. The less excitement he has the better, that goes without saying of course.'

She almost gasped as his cool gaze raked her, implying that he thought, quite clearly, that she was a bad influence on Gray and obviously couldn't wait to remove him from her clutches. Biting back her fury she lowered her head, searching for a note pad, anything rather than see the contempt which she knew would be in his eyes.

'I understand, Doctor.' Her pen was poised over the paper. 'You wish the patient to travel by sea.'

'That's right. I know it will take longer but I'd rather avoid any risk of pressure on the eyes. I shall arrange for an ambulance to meet the ferry at St Malo and a car to drive him straight from there to the château.'

She frowned. 'Not to the clinic?'

'Not immediately.'

'But . . . I understood you wished to do more tests.'

'That is so, Sister, but they can be carried out equally well in the patient's own environment and he will be happier there where everything is familiar.' He flung the file onto the desk. 'I'm leaving it to Mr Westlake to arrange with Danielle, Mr Masterson's ward, for nursing care, since I don't have time. At this stage of course it will be minimal, but necessary all the same. He's still suffering from concussion and until we know exactly what else we're up against I'm not taking any chances.' His mouth tightened. 'I wish I could stay and travel back with him personally.'

Clare felt her heart thud. 'I'm sure your wishes can be carried out perfectly satisfactorily, Doctor, and you said yourself there's very little that can be done at this stage.' She glanced at him. 'But what about later?'

The dark eyes scanned her face. 'I take it your interest is purely professional rather than personal?'

'Naturally,' she lied, wondering whether he would have answered had she admitted the truth.

'Then you must know it's too early to say. I was telling Gray the truth.'

'I realise that, Doctor, but you examined him. Briefly I know, but you must have come to some conclusion.'

There was a moment's hesitation which was somehow so alien to him that she found it disconcerting. 'I'm not happy about things. We could be up against any number of possibilities and even you must realise that we can't entirely discount a tumour.'

Clare felt herself sway and was suddenly aware of his hand on her arm. She knew that the colour had drained from her face but somehow she managed to recover herself and found herself looking up into the handsome but frowning face.

'Are you all right, Sister?'

'I . . .' she swallowed hard. 'Yes, perfectly thank you, Doctor. The heat in here . . . the office is rather small.' Her head was reeling. Surely fate couldn't be so hideously cruel, not to Gray?

She found herself released but there was a look of disapproval remaining in his eyes. 'Did you eat a proper meal before coming on duty, or like so many other females are you too busy counting calories? It's a ridiculous habit, especially for someone in your job, and you of all people should know better.'

Clare forced a smile to her lips. 'You're right of course, Doctor.' Let him think what he liked. 'I'll get something to eat later. I have a break round about midnight.' She was conscious of the hand he had removed from her arm, strong, capable, yet amazingly gentle.

'See that you do then, Sister. You look as if you need feeding up.'

Really, he was too much. What right had he to intrude into her personal life? 'Was there anything else, Doctor?' She put the desk between them and, irrationally, felt safer. What was it about him that made her feel so vulnerable?

'I don't think so. The ambulance and nursing escort should be fully equipped to deal with every contingency. I'll make sure a cabin is reserved on board and tickets will be reserved to await collection. I'll leave a letter for Miss Neuville giving all the details, perhaps you'll see that she gets it?'

'Naturally. I'll see to it.'

'Fine. I think that's it, apart from the notes which Mr Westlake was kind enough to agree to my having.'

She held out a slim file with Gray's name on it. 'I have them here.'

She was glad when he simply took them and left. Suddenly the tiny office seemed large and very empty.

'. . . not that I'm really objecting. On the contrary.'

Gray's voice brought her back to the present with a jolt and she turned to the narrow bed in the cabin where he was lying. He was pale and a pang of remorse ran through her. 'I'm sorry, Gray, you were saying something.'

His mouth twisted. 'I was saying you don't have to stay here nurse-maiding me every minute of the day and night, not that I'm objecting you understand.'

Clare laughed. 'I know I don't have to stay. I choose to, unless you'd rather I left you to get some rest. You do look tired.'

'I suppose I am, but I seem to have spent enough time sleeping just lately. No,' his hand reached out and she took it. 'Don't go. I'm being selfish, Clare, I know that, but I find it hard to believe this is really happening. I keep thinking I shall wake up and it will all have been a wretched dream.'

'I know, Gray.' Her hand tightened over his. 'I do know, but try not to upset yourself. Everything's going to be all right. You'll be home soon.'

He lay back against the pillows as if the mere effort of speaking had exhausted him. 'You're the only good thing that's come out of this whole, stinking business. I don't know what I'd have done without you.'

Her throat felt tight. 'You would have been all right. Someone else would have taken care of you just as well as I could.'

'But I don't want anyone else. I want you.' He turned his head in her direction. 'You're not going to run out on me again, are you, little mouse?'

Sitting on the edge of the bed, Clare felt the tremor of excitement run through her. 'Don't worry. I'll stay with you, at least for as long as you need me. But you're going to get well again.'

'Am I?' He laughed bitterly. 'I wish I could see that pretty face of yours, see the expression in your eyes.' He pulled her closer and his hands went to her face, moving gently over her eyes and hair, the soft roundness of her cheeks, then, before she knew what was happening, he had drawn her down and kissed her lightly on her lips. It was a gentle kiss at first and then, as if sensing that there was no resistance it became more searching, almost as if he was trying to learn something his eyes couldn't tell him. There was a kind of desperation in him. Clare recognised it and its cause and her mouth responded, softening beneath his. Gray wasn't the only one for whom things were like a dream. Her head was reeling. She was in Gray's arms but this was real, very real, and she didn't want the reality to end.

She surfaced, flushed and breathless, conscious of the crumpled state of her uniform but hardly caring. Her voice caught in her throat. 'I don't think that was such a good idea. I'm supposed to be making sure you don't get over-excited.'

'Am I the only one, Clare?' He seemed reluctant to let her go completely. 'Was the excitement all mine or did I just imagine that you actually enjoyed it too?'

She was glad he couldn't see her face as she got to her feet, tucking escaping strands of hair under her cap. 'No, you didn't imagine it, Gray, but I shouldn't have let it happen. I'm supposed to be your nurse and I hardly think Dr Duval would approve.' In fact she was certain of it.

'Alain?' His laughter was deep-throated. 'I don't give a damn what Alain approves or disapproves. He may be responsible for my health but not my personal life. Oh I know he can breathe fire, but you don't have to take any notice.'

No, she thought, except that I'm the one likely to be scorched in the blast, and in any case she was genuinely alarmed to see the pallor creep back into Gray's face as he closed his eyes again briefly. Her fingers went automatically to his wrist feeling the pulse. 'Are you all right?'

'Yes, I'm fine, don't fuss, there's a girl. It's just this headache.'

'I'll give you some tablets, they should fix it.' She crossed to her bag, shook two tablets from a bottle and poured a little water, helping him to take them. Afterwards he lay quietly, his hand imprisoning hers.

'I can scarcely believe my luck, you know that? If I have to be stuck with a nurse at all, I'm glad it's you and not some pewter-haired matron without a heart.'

'I may not be a matron,' she assured him softly, 'but you may as well get used to the idea here and now, I mean to keep you in order, so you'd better behave, Gray Masterson.'

'And take my medicine like a good little boy?' There was a sharpness in his tone, then it was gone as he laughed. 'Don't worry, I won't give you a hard time, at least not in the way you mean. But in others . . . I warn you, Sister, I can't make the same promise, so you'd better watch out. I may not be able to see, but I don't plan to let that inhibit me too much and when I do get my sight back . . .'

She drew in a deep breath and released it shakily. The words seemed to cut into her heart holding a bitter irony of which he, mercifully, was unaware. She managed to say lightly, 'Well thanks for the warning, but just remember it isn't proper for a nurse to flirt with her patient.'

His head turned restlessly in her direction. 'I wasn't thinking in terms of a mild flirtation.' He frowned and she saw the two spots of colour heightening in his cheeks. 'But of course I forgot, I may not be much of a catch. I should have realised . . . I mean, who would want to tie themselves to a blind man?'

With a gasp of horror she knelt beside him. 'That wasn't what I meant, Gray. How could you even think it?'

For a moment he was tight-lipped. 'Why not? It takes some getting used to, even for me.'

'But you won't have to get used to it.'

'Oh Clare, sweet Clare, you can't say that with absolute certainty can you? Can you?' he pressed.

'I . . .' She blinked the tears away quickly but his fingers had already felt them on her cheeks and he shook her gently.

'Don't, please, not for me. I just want to know . . . if it happens . . . would you still be here? I don't think I could bear to lose you.' His fingers gripped even more possessively, hurting her, but she made no attempt to free them. He was tense, like a coiled spring and she could feel the pulse beating in his wrist.

'I'd still be here, Gray, whatever happens. As long as you want me to stay.'

She felt him relax and sat with him until he fell into an uneasy sleep. There was something almost frightening about the way in which he had clung to her promise, finding reassurance in it. She bent to kiss him gently on the cheek. He was like a sick child, vulnerable and afraid, turning to someone for comfort and she had been able to give it.

It hardly seemed possible after all these years when she had only dreamed of Gray, that now she had found him and he had asked her to stay. He needed her. Perhaps it wasn't love, not yet, but one day . . .

Alain Duval wouldn't approve of course, but that was a bridge she would cross if and when she came to it. She didn't know why thoughts of the mocking features should suddenly intrude into her mind and didn't care. But as she let herself quietly out of the cabin and went to get some fresh air up on deck, it was infuriating to find that they remained stubbornly with her and she began to dread the next, inevitable encounter.

CHAPTER FOUR

THE ambulance was waiting as they docked at St Malo. Clare saw it from the deck where she had been standing as the ferry drew in and she hurried down to the cabin now to ensure that everything was ready for Gray to be taken off. He was awake but rather pale and it was with a feeling of disquiet that she watched as he was carried by two attendants out to the waiting vehicle. In fact, the manoeuvre was carried out without complications since they had been advised to wait until the rest of the passengers and their cars had disembarked and the dock was virtually deserted as she walked beside the stretcher towards the ambulance, apart from the sleek, black limousine which was parked close by.

Clare's glance lingered on it for a moment. It was the kind of car one dreamed about, expensive, luxurious, made for travelling in comfort. Whoever the owner was he must be rich she thought, without any sense of envy. It was a lifestyle entirely different from her own.

Danielle, however, gasped with delight and rushed on ahead. 'Oh look, Alain's car. Bless him, he is such an angel.'

Clare's eyes drifted with dismay to the solitary, distant figure, leaning nonchalantly against the car, and felt her mouth suddenly become dry. Oh no, it couldn't be. She had hoped at least to get Gray safely installed at the château before having to face the inevitable confrontation with Dr Alain Duval.

The figure moved as she drew closer and she noted the greying hair. Her heartbeat steadied. The man wore a chauffeur's uniform and for some reason she didn't even try to interpret, she felt perversely disappointed.

She was given no time to dwell on it, however, as, with a tinge of annoyance she saw Danielle slide into the front seat of the huge car, leaving Clare not only to supervise Gray's safe installation into the ambulance but the stowing of all their luggage into the vast car boot as well. Through the back window she saw Danielle adjusting her lipstick and flicking a comb through her hair. The chauffeur met Clare's gaze and grinned sympathetically as he relieved her of her own rather battered suitcase and managed to find a space for it. Blushing for the fact that her thoughts must have been so obvious, she muttered '*Merci*' and sped back to the waiting ambulance, climbed in and took a seat opposite to where Gray was lying.

She was a little concerned about him as they moved off. He was pale but when she asked if his head was still troubling him it was almost a relief to hear him admit that it wasn't his head but the damaged leg which was aching. Almost routinely she felt for his pulse and he smiled, weakly.

'Still fussing over me, Clare. You'll have to

watch it. It might become a habit. One I could get too used to.'

Her voice caught in her throat as she stared down at him. With an effort she managed to inject a note of lightness in her voice. 'Don't worry, there won't be time for it to develop into a habit. You'll be well again before you know it. In any case, I have a job to go back to in England, you know.'

'Perhaps I could offer you a better one over here.'

She smiled. 'Yes, well for now the job I'm doing is quite sufficient and I'm not going to be diverted from it by any amount of talk. Sleep now.' Her voice was purposely firm and she was relieved to see that he closed his eyes without protest.

The ambulance moved quickly and smoothly over the roads, eating up mile after mile of French countryside, and gradually Gray's features relaxed and she knew by his even breathing that he was asleep. Watching him, seeing the strange vulnerability which it seemed to lend to his features, Clare felt a surge of despondency grip her. Her job was going to be hard enough as it was. She would simply have to remind herself that she was here for one reason and one reason only, to work. Gray was just a patient and she mustn't become involved, but the way he talked didn't make things any easier.

She turned to stare out of the darkened windows, glad to see again places she remembered. St Malo with vast stretches of sands which, in summer, would be golden and filled with tourists, but now the sea was bleak and pewter-grey, yet Clare found herself wishing there was time to walk along the beach, feeling the wind blowing in her hair, breathing in the cold air, perhaps with someone beside her. A shadowy figure. She frowned as an image of Alain Duval pushed its way infuriatingly into her mind.

With an effort of concentration she switched her gaze to the cobbled streets and the town's ramparts which should have been old but were in fact mostly quite new. The war had destroyed a lot of history in the beautiful town, but not all. There were still ancient walls and granite houses to be seen.

Moving along the coast they passed through Dinard with its old church and the turreted house in the Grande Rue, called the Black Prince's Lodge. Clare breathed deeply. She had always loved history and France in particular seemed to draw her, weaving a spell from which there was no escape once it had been experienced, and the feeling of age and the splendour of bygone eras was even greater as they reached Dinard. The town stood high on a crag above the river. There were still the remains of the castle where Anne de Bretagne, Queen of Charles the Third, had often come to stay.

The light was beginning to fade as they passed quaint buildings with roofs of so many varied and beautiful shapes, like picturesque fairy castles from a child's story book. The market in the busy town square, with its fruit and vegetables and cages of young ducklings, a goat. People from outlying villages and farmsteads all bringing their goods to be sold.

It was snowing quite heavily by the time they reached the château and was almost dark, yet not too dark to see it silhouetted against the skyline as they turned into the long, tree-lined drive. Clare felt her breath quicken with excitement and glanced down quickly at Gray. He was still asleep and she was glad he couldn't see the flush in her cheeks. If only she could have been coming here as his wife.

She drew herself up sharply, angry with herself for falling so easily into the trap again. She was here only to help him get well and when that happened her usefulness here would be ended. Or would it? Gray seemed to need her, to want her to stay, but she might be in danger of mistaking his motives. Clare bit her lip as her gaze went to the familiar features and felt as if something tugged at her heartstrings. Dear, dear Gray, whatever happened, for the moment she was with him, despite Alain Duval, and that was all that mattered. The future could take care of itself.

Their arrival was obviously expected. As the car drew up the door of the château was already opening and Clare was vaguely aware of figures moving down the steps and taking the stretcher which bore Gray into the brightly-lit warmth beyond. Danielle followed, furs clutched round her as the icy wind hit them full force. Her face was taut and she barely acknowledged the housekeeper's greeting before hurrying up the wide, ornate staircase after Gray.

The woman's face lit up as she recognised Clare. 'Ah, mademoiselle. It is good to see you again. It has been a long time, too long.'

'And it's good to see you again too.' Clare stopped, smiling, as she shrugged herself out of her navy coat. She was cold and tired and there was a great deal of work to be done before she could relax, but it was good to see a familiar face and to know that she was remembered. 'I only wish it could be under different circumstances.' She shivered and the woman frowned.

'I will 'ave some 'ot food made ready.'

'That would be very nice.' Clare nodded her appreciation of the thought. 'But I'd better see to my patient first.' Her shoes echoed on the marble tiled floor as she crossed the hall and hurried up the stairs. It had been five years but nothing had changed. Her feet unerringly found their way and she felt an odd sense of exhilaration that her memory hadn't played her false.

Gray was in bed when she quietly entered his room. Danielle was sitting in the chair beside him, still wearing her coat, her face white with exhaustion, yet, for one brief moment as she entered the room, Clare sensed a flicker of animosity in the girl's eyes. It was gone so quickly that she told herself she must have imagined it.

'He looks so pale.' Danielle rose to her feet and stared down at the still figure.

Clare automatically lifted Gray's wrist as it lay against the covers, feeling the pulse. It was reassuringly steady. 'He'll be all right,' she said. 'As a matter of fact he's stood up to the journey very well, but he needs plenty of sleep and rest during the next few days before he undergoes any more tests.'

'I'd like to stay with him for a while.'

'I'd rather you didn't.'

Spots of angry colour highlighted Danielle's cheeks as she stared, tightlipped, at Clare. 'You have no right to refuse me. You forget, we are not at your hospital now. This is my home and you are employed only as a nurse.'

Shock held Clare rigid. She didn't know how, but somehow she managed to face the girl, recognising the sense of helplessness they were both sharing even if her own couldn't be put into words. 'Exactly,' her voice was gentle. 'I am a nurse and I am here because you asked me to come, for no other reason.'

The beautiful eyes narrowed then filled with tears as she stifled a sob. 'Please, forgive me. I am distraught. This isn't the Gray I know.'

Clare went to her quickly, putting an arm about her shoulders. 'I know,' she said, softly. 'Believe me, I do understand, but you're exhausted too. You've had a nasty shock and it isn't over yet, but there is nothing you can do here. I'm going to give Gray his medication and see that he is settled for the night. The tablets will help him sleep so why don't you go and do the same. Have some hot food and go to bed. Marguerite was preparing some soup and coffee.'

Danielle sighed, pushing a strand of pale hair

from her eyes. 'I know you are right, but I feel so useless.'

'That's nonsense. There will be a great deal you can do, but later. For the moment the best help you can give Gray is to get some sleep so that you are fresh and able to cope when he needs company.' Her face clouded. 'It could take a long time, Danielle. You'll need your strength and so will I.' She was relieved to see the girl's attempt at a smile.

'Yes, I am tired. I shall do as you say, but you will call me . . . ?'

'If there is any need of course I will. But there won't be.' Gently she urged the girl towards the door and Danielle paused.

'I have given you the room next to Gray's. I thought it best. I'm afraid it isn't what you had before, when you spent the holidays here, in fact it's little more than a dressing room . . .'

'Please, don't worry. It will be fine. I shall be able to hear if Gray wakes and needs anything.' She smiled and closed the door behind Danielle, leaning against it for a moment as yet another reminder that she was not here as a guest gradually sank into her brain. Dully she crossed to her small case in which she carried Gray's notes and medication and, sitting at a small table, she began to write.

Only later, when she was certain he was sleeping peacefully, did she make her way downstairs to the hall where the family took their meals. Here too, in spite of five years' absence, she was glad to see that nothing had changed either. The same faces still looked down at her from the portraits hung on the walls, coldly indifferent to her solitary presence. She stared up at them and one face in particular sent a sudden tremor running through her. A man, dressed in the costume of the sixteenth century, dark eyed, the aquiline features had an arrogance which reminded her uncannily of someone else. It was the face of a man who knew what he wanted and would not baulk at doing what he had to do to get it. In spite of the ruffed collar, the padded sleeves and dark, velvet cloak, it was as if Alain Duval stood there, taunting her with his own power. For some reason it left her feeling vulnerable and she purposely turned away to go and stand by the huge log fire.

Although she was tired she was surprised to find that in fact she was quite hungry and she ate the food the housekeeper was kind enough to bring to her on a tray. Marguerite stood over her, chattering as Clare savoured the exquisitely flavoured fish soup, followed by an omelette cooked as she remembered only Marguerite could cook them. Her plate empty at last she sat back sipping at her coffee and the woman's face wreathed in smiles.

'You should eat more. While you are here Marguerite will put some fat on those bones.' She clucked fussily and Clare laughed.

'I'm sure you will. Too much if I'm not careful.'

'*Mais non*, you have the appetite like *un petit oiseau*, the little bird.'

Stifling a yawn Clare got to her feet. 'Well, this little bird is going to bed. It's been a long day and I shall be up early again tomorrow.'

'Sleep well, mademoiselle.' The housekeeper gathered up the tray. 'I will have the *petit dejeuner* sent up to your room.'

'Oh no,' Clare said, hastily. 'I'm here to work, not to be treated as a guest. I'll come down.'

'Then there will be *café et croissants* waiting,' the woman said, firmly, then, as she turned to go she nodded towards the small writing desk. 'I forgot, *Monsieur le docteur*, 'e leave the telephone number, in case 'e should be needed.'

Clare crossed to the table, extracting a brief note from the envelope. The handwriting was large and the wording of the message decisive. Just like the man himself, she thought, with an irrational stab of resentment.

'Should you need me urgently, do not hesitate to call this number, day or night, otherwise I shall make my first visit tomorrow.'

'Perish the thought', Clare murmured under her breath as she pocketed the card. 'Let sleeping giants lie.' Saying goodnight to the housekeeper she made her way at last to bed, but it was some time before she fell asleep.

CHAPTER FIVE

CLARE woke early the next morning and lay for some seconds trying to recall where she was. Memory returned and had her swiftly pushing back the covers and shrugging herself into a warm dressing gown. The château didn't boast central heating and the fire which had been lit the previous evening in her room was reduced to the pale white ash of burned logs.

Shivering she hurried to Gray's room. To her relief he was still sleeping peacefully and some of the colour had returned to his face, but the still uncanny resemblance to a little boy brought a lump to her throat.

Leaving him to sleep on she returned to her room, showered, dressed out of habit in a clean, navy dress and perched a frilled cap on her head, tucking any stray wisps of hair neatly out of sight. Her expression stared back at her from the glass, the mouth just a shade too large, the eyes an indefinible grey-green at this moment, not the kind a man could drown in, she thought, wryly, especially a man like Alain Duval. Her hands tightened spasmodically at the belt encircling her waist as she realised that her thoughts had taken a totally unwarranted and certainly undesirable track. Blast the man, why did he have to keep intruding where he wasn't welcome? It was going to be bad enough when they came face to face in the flesh again without having him force himself into her thoughts as well.

She made her way downstairs and across the hall, but instead of going directly to the dining room, made her way to the door, slipping out to stand for a few moments on the steps.

The bite of the snow-laden air took her breath away and she clasped her arms involuntarily about her own body, but it was the view which held her speechless as she stared at snow-covered trees which lined a drive, as yet unmarred by any human footprint. A squirrel scuttled in front of her, eyed her in some surprise and darted away up into the branches sending a shower of flakes cascading down. It was beautiful. Even more so now than it had been in summer. There was a fairy-tale quality about it all, and a rare sense of depression brought the tears to cloud her eyes as she remembered that Gray wouldn't be able to see it.

Reluctantly she went in and ate croissants, still warm from the oven, liberally spread with apricot preserve, and drank several cups of coffee before making her way back to Gray's room.

He stirred as she entered and she spoke, realising how easy it was for a fully sighted person to take it for granted that a blind one would automatically know who was there.

'Good morning. How are you feeling? You slept well.'

'Did I?' As he fought his way from the depths of

sleep she put the tray she had brought with her onto the bedside table and made the routine tests of pulse and temperature. He bore it silently and she noticed the faint stubble on his chin, making a mental note to arrange for a valet to be in attendance to deal with the simple matters of shaving and bathing which had, almost overnight, become not so simple. A patient's dignity was every bit as important as his general health and well-being. It was something which had been constantly drilled into them in Training School, but only now was the full significance driven home. Gray was a man who valued his independence. The fact that some things he would now find impossible to do for himself was a problem she would have to tackle slowly and tactfully. For all she was a trained nurse, having a man to perform such necessary and personal functions for him would be a first step. She would talk to Danielle and see if young Pierre Lescour, one of the men who worked in the household, could be spared for an hour or so each day.

'How's the headache this morning?'

'Not so bad. As a matter of fact not bad at all, more like a dull ache.'

'That's good. I'm sure the doctor will be pleased when he comes later.' She put the breakfast tray on the bed in front of him. 'Can you manage? I must arrange to have a proper over-bed table . . .'

'Of course I can manage. For God's sake, don't fuss,' he rasped. 'I'm not totally blind yet you know. There are still shadows.'

Clare drew back, biting at her lip. 'I realise that. I

simply meant are you comfortable? Shall I re-
arrange your pillows for you?'

'Sorry.' He frowned. 'I suppose I'm a bit touchy.
It's all the waiting. I'd rather know what's going to
happen. The sooner they find out the sooner I can
start adjusting, though God knows to what.'

She kept her voice deliberately cheerful. 'Well,
Dr Duval will be along later and I imagine he'll
have some news of when they want to go ahead with
the tests. He may even have had the results of some
of the others.' She busied herself about the room,
talking as she moved so that he would be able to
follow her movements as he ate. 'I expect you'll
want to have a shave and a bath.'

A piece of buttered croissant was held poised
halfway to his mouth. 'You're not thinking of
volunteering?'

'Actually, no.' She smiled gently to herself and
saw his mouth contort.

'Ah, pity.'

'As a matter of fact I was going to suggest that
Pierre take over each morning, perhaps while I
have my own breakfast and before I bring you
yours, just to help you dress.'

A knife clattered to the plate and his voice
hardened. 'It's not necessary. I'm quite capable of
taking a shower alone. I've been doing it for a long
time.'

'Yes, I know, and I'm not suggesting that you're
incapable now. What I'm advising is that Pierre
should be somewhere close at hand, just in case.'

'Just in case what . . .?'

Clare bit back a response knowing she must temper pity with firmness. 'It's a sensible precaution, Gray. One which would be taken in any hospital, if only you'll think about it, so please, do just that. Think it before you reject the idea out of hand. You still have a slight concussion. You might become dizzy or get one of your headaches.' She broke off. 'You must learn to accept help when it is offered, Gray. There's nothing wrong with it, it isn't a sign of weakness. It simply means you'll learn to cope so much more quickly. In any case as long as I'm here, I'm responsible and I'd be failing in my duties if I allowed you to take such a risk.' Her chin rose. 'So make your choice, Pierre or me.'

He put the tray aside, staring in the direction of her voice. 'I don't really have much choice, do I?'

'No, not much.' Her pulse-rate steadied as he seemed resigned. 'Look, how about getting up for a while? Do you feel up to it?'

'You mean I'm allowed?'

'I wouldn't suggest it if you weren't. As a matter of fact Dr Duval is keen that you should. We don't have patients lying around in their beds these days, you know. Even after major surgery we get them up within hours.'

'In that case why are we waiting?' He swung his feet slowly over the side of the bed and she went to help.

'Here, lean on me, you're still weak after the accident. Don't do anything too quickly, everything nice and easy, there's plenty of time.'

'You're a bully, you know that?' His face was

close to her own and his arm tightened around her shoulders. She was glad to hear the lightness in his voice and her heart quivered as he leaned against her. She swallowed hard.

'If you mean I intend getting my own way, then yes, you're right. Easy now. Sit down again for a minute and get your breath back.'

He obeyed, sitting on the bed breathing hard. She saw the thin film of sweat on his face. 'God, I feel as useless as a kitten.'

'That's natural after being in bed. You'll find you get a little stronger each day as you move around. How's the leg?'

'A damn nuisance.' His hand probed the bandages. 'Not bad really, though I think I'm going to need a little help to get up again.'

'That's what I'm here for.' She slipped her arm around his waist and he hauled himself up to stand in front of her, but instead of releasing her as she expected, he made no attempt to do so. Instead she found herself held, her heart thudding wildly, as his hand rose and began to trace the contours of her cheek.

He frowned. 'I was right, you are beautiful. The ugly little duckling turned out to be a swan, not that this particular duckling was ever ugly.' His fingers moved to her hair and she closed her eyes, feeling that the whole situation was getting out of hand.

'Gray . . . I have work to do,' she said, weakly. 'You'd better let me go before someone comes in. This isn't at all ethical.'

He laughed, softly. 'Who cares? Tell me, little

swan, what colour is your hair? Auburn? I'm sure it was auburn. I can see a faint smudge of colour.'

Her mouth felt dry. So many times she had imagined being in his arms yet now, when it happened, her voice died in her throat and her legs felt like jelly. 'Actually I'm afraid it's brown, just plain, good old-fashioned brown.' Why did she feel she had to apologise for the fact?

'There's nothing wrong with brown,' his fingers moved again, this time to her mouth and before she knew what was happening he had drawn her to him and his lips came down on her own, cutting off the cry of surprise before it rose.

It wasn't a gentle kiss as she had imagined it would be. It was demanding and her head reeled from the sheer pressure and unexpectedness of it. It was crazy too. Even as her lips responded traitorously she reminded herself that Gray was her patient, that she should never have allowed this to happen, not here, not like this. 'No Gray, don't, please.' She managed to free her mouth long enough to murmur the words, heard his own, muffled, against her hair.

'Darling Clare. I've waited such a long time.' Before he claimed her mouth again.

With a sense of impending doom she was aware of the door opening behind her and knew that someone stood there. With a supreme effort she dragged herself away from Gray, her hand going to her cap which had become dislodged and sending her hair tumbling in wild disorder. She knew that her cheeks were brilliant with colour but it drained instantly as she turned to stare into the familiar face which studied her now with such angry contempt. The dark eyes of Alain Duval blazed as he stepped into the room and Clare flinched as she saw recognition dawn disbelievingly.

'You?'

She gulped, wishing the earth would open and swallow her up. The arrogant gaze flicked her from head to toe and she saw his mouth tighten as he made his judgment of the situation. She wanted to tell him that it wasn't what he thought, but the words wouldn't come and even if they had, she had the feeling that this man would never believe her, especially when Gray's hand moved to her shoulder again.

She evaded it, not daring to lift her own gaze to that of the waiting man. Of all the people who might have come through that door at that precise moment it had to be him, she groaned inwardly. It wasn't as if she had even invited Gray's kiss, if she had it might have been different, but as it was this man had already dared to judge her and find her guilty. She licked her lips. It was no excuse. Somehow she should have prevented it happening. The blame was hers and Alain Duval knew it.

His voice when he spoke was icy and measured. 'I think some explanations are necessary, Sister. No,' he cut her off, 'not now. I have a patient to see. Later. For the moment I suggest you remove yourself while I make the examination.'

Something, a desire to salvage what little dignity

she could from the situation, made her draw herself up and face him.

'In case you had forgotten, Doctor, I am a fully qualified nurse.'

The steely gaze returned to her as he put his bag on the table. 'No, I hadn't forgotten, Sister, but I thought you must have done.' The dark eyes narrowed. 'I wonder, do you give all your male patients an equal share of your . . . skills?'

Anger brought the colour flooding to her face but she was denied even the satisfaction of a reply as he turned abruptly away to give his attention to Gray, who, to her intense relief, seemed to have been mercifully unaware of their low interchange.

He sat on the bed now, rigid with tension, his face pale as he waited and she found herself marvelling at the obvious pleasure with which he greeted the man who was, in her opinion, nothing but an arrogant, male chauvinist pig.

The fact that he conducted the examination in a deceptively easy manner, offering Gray just the right amount of reassurance yet doing what had to be done even though it involved a certain amount of discomfort, did however draw from Clare a certain, grudging admiration, and her responses were purely automatic as she handed first the drops which were to be inserted into Gray's eyes in order to make the examination easier, and then the ophthalmoscope with which the actual examination would be carried out. She felt her heart go out to Gray, knowing what was at stake and realising that he must be aware of it too. She found herself watching Alain Duval's expression for some hint of what he found, but it revealed nothing, not that she had really expected otherwise. He was too good at judging other people's actions to betray any of his own, she thought, and, with an even greater sense of irritation, noted that the large, tanned hands, for all their size, were amazingly gentle.

It was over before even she was fully aware of it and she set about the immediate task of clearing away the used equipment, carrying the tray into the adjoining room which had been fitted out in the little time which had been available as a storage room for dressings and other necessary equipment and medications. Glad of an excuse to escape she prolonged her absence for as long as possible, half hoping he would leave without having to face him again. As she worked she listened but caught only muffled sounds through the half open door. She hated to return yet she had to find out whether there was, as yet, any clearer picture of what was wrong with Gray.

The sight of the tall figure standing in the doorway as she turned took her by surprise so that she dropped a steel dish, sending it clattering to the floor. Bending to retrieve it she was conscious yet again of the look of contempt as he added yet another black mark to his undoubtedly already growing list. She didn't know what it was about him that seemed to have the effect of making her appear clumsy and inefficient when in reality she was neither of those things, far from it. But it was the knowledge that those weren't the only sins he laid at her door which really rankled.

'I'm sorry, Doctor, I didn't see you standing there. You made me jump. I thought you must have left.'

He walked in, closing the door behind him, making the room seem suddenly even smaller. 'I'm sorry to disappoint you . . . Sister, but I thought I had made it clear that I had no intention of leaving until I have some answers.'

Clare caught her breath. 'I don't understand, Doctor.'

'Oh I think you do.' Anger flashed briefly in the dark eyes. 'I think you know very well what I mean. Let's start with how you happen to be here at all. It certainly wasn't by my orders. Quite the contrary, if I'd known . . .'

'You would have refused me?' Clare felt her temper rising and fought to control it. 'But on what grounds?'

He laughed, bitterly. 'I think the little episode which greeted me this morning when I arrived so unexpectedly saves the need for any further discussion.'

'But . . . that's totally unfair.'

'You deny what happened?' His brow rose.

'Well . . . no. But it wasn't what you thought.'

'You don't know what I thought.'

'No, but I can imagine,' she said through gritted teeth, 'and I would like it to be understood that I do not make a habit of . . . fraternising with my patients, doctor. What happened was . . .'

'Unfortunate?' He was mocking her. 'Yes, it

was, to say the least. But it alters nothing. It doesn't explain why you are here and I'm still waiting for an explanation. I take it you do have one.'

She clenched her hands together against a desire to slap the arrogant face, guessing uneasily that any such action would undoubtedly bring a speedy and painful retaliation. She didn't credit Alain Duval with the manners of a gentleman.

'You gave no specific orders as to who should accompany Gr . . . the patient and as I knew him, and Mademoiselle Neuville anyway, and she asked me if I would consider taking the job, I saw no reason to refuse.'

Her chin rose as she saw anger sweep across the dark face. 'Are you sure that's the only reason?'

'But of course, what else?'

'What else indeed?' His mouth twisted. 'You don't, I suppose, hold any romantic notions towards the patient which might have influenced your decision? Gray Masterson is a very rich man and at this moment a very vulnerable one. It would be very easy . . .'

She didn't let him finish. This time the hand she had been holding in check found its mark leaving a brilliant weal across his cheek. She stared at it, and at him, aghast, but instead of the retaliation she had expected his eyes narrowed.

'That may relieve your feelings. It doesn't answer the question, or does it?'

She paused, breathing heavily. 'I don't see that my private life is any concern of yours . . . Doctor.'

'You're right, it isn't, unless it impinges upon

your work and there seems to be a grave danger of it doing so. I simply feel the need to warn you, not only for your own sake, but for the patient's as well.'

'What do you mean?' Her gaze wavered. 'Have you found out anything, have the tests shown something?'

The sensual mouth tightened. 'You may as well know that I'm not entirely happy about Gray's condition. The damage caused by the accident was relatively minor, almost non-existent, and what there was has almost healed.'

Clare stared at him with a sense of cold desperation. 'I don't understand. Gray can't see, or at least very little. There has to be a reason. If not the accident then what?'

'Of course there is a reason.' Alain Duval moved to sit on the edge of the table facing her. 'I suspect that Gray had been getting the headaches for some time and that they had gradually been getting worse. I also think that his eyesight must have been affected, though he chose not to admit it. That may have caused the accident.'

'Oh no.' Clare felt the sudden sinking in the pit of her stomach. 'But why would he want to keep it a secret? What possible reason could there be?'

'Who knows?' The muscular shoulders were raised in a shrug. 'Gray is an artist. Perhaps he was afraid people would say he was losing his touch. He may not have wanted to admit it even to himself or it's possible the loss of vision was so incipient that he may genuinely have been unaware of it in the beginning. It isn't gone completely, you must have noticed that for yourself?'

'Yes.' Her voice was little more than a whisper. 'But what about the tests?'

'The results we've had so far discount any possibility of a tumour.'

'Oh, thank God.'

'As you say, thank God, but it doesn't mean we're out of the woods yet, far from it. There are several possibilities, all of them are going to be difficult for a man like Gray to accept. Whatever happens he's going to need the support of someone he cares for.'

'You mean . . . he may become totally blind?'

'It's a possibility we can't discount. I'm hoping it won't be the case. I have my own theories, but at this stage that's all they are. We shan't know for certain until an operation has been performed and I'm loath to do that until he's fully recovered from the shock and other effects of the accident.'

Clare felt her head spinning. 'You say you have theories. What theories?' She knew her voice was shrill but couldn't prevent the note of panic.

'Several, but one in particular. I gather Gray was abroad for some time recently and picked up a pretty bad dose of malaria. I'm concentrating on that, but the accident complicated things a little. The retinal vessels are extremely contracted and the disc is pale.'

'But if your suspicions are right, what then?'

'An operation is a certainty.'

'And just how serious is it?' His face was little

more than a blur in front of her.

He was silent for a moment as he studied her. 'I won't pretend it's simple. As a nurse you must know the risks, but I've every reason to believe it will be a success.'

'And if it isn't?'

'Then there is a chance he may lose his sight altogether.'

She knew she was staring at him, that she should say something, anything, but somehow the words wouldn't come. The room was beginning to spin. It couldn't happen to Gray, not Gray.

Her head was lowered as she breathed deeply, fighting a wave of blackness, then as she swayed an arm suddenly went round her, supporting her in such a way that she allowed herself to lean gratefully against the strong, muscular body. Her hand pressed against her mouth.

'Breathe deeply.' The voice was terse, almost brutal, and it was enough to bring her up with a start. Her head jerked up and even though her eyes were closed she felt a sudden awareness of his strength and the maleness of him envelop her. The smell of his jacket, a subtle waft of after-shave. Her hand froze against his chest where his jacket was open. Her eyes flew open and she stared into the taut face above her own before he stiffened and for one incredible moment a sense of weakness assailed her body. It was utterly crazy. She gave herself a mental shake, fighting to release herself from his grasp, but his hands retained their hold on her, almost as if he were afraid that if he let her go she would fall into a lifeless heap at his feet. The thought was echoed by the look of contempt which suddenly contorted the handsome features.

'Are you always this emotional where your patients are concerned? If so, then I would suggest that you're in the wrong profession, Sister. In nursing one needs to learn how to become dispassionate.'

Her gaze flew angrily to his. 'I'm sure your sentiments are sound, Doctor. Unfortunately we can't all be as cold blooded as you.'

'Then perhaps you should learn,' he said, roughly. 'Your patient doesn't need pity, neither yours nor anyone elses, least of all mine. That isn't going to make him well and if you haven't realised that by now then you won't do your job efficiently and it would be better for everyone's sake if you just packed your bags here and now and went back to England.'

The sheer callousness of the words made her gasp. 'I'm not offering Gray pity, Doctor, but I can give him sympathy. There is a subtle difference and surely even you can't disapprove of that?'

'On the contrary, I disapprove of anything which is likely to impede the progress of my patient.'

'Gray isn't just any patient.' She flung the words at him and saw the warning glint in his eyes.

'No? Then what, Sister, perhaps you'll enlighten me.'

'I . . .' She bit her lip, hating him for the ease with which he seemed able to tear down all her defences. 'Gray happens to be a friend of mine.'

'He also happens to be a friend of mine, but I don't feel the need to resort to hysterics.'

The muscles knotted in her throat. 'I am not hysterical.' To her chagrin she felt the tears prick at her eyes. This man was insufferable. What business was it of his what her relationship with Gray might be? Yet his expression said clearly enough that he had drawn his own conclusions and nothing she could say or do would change them.

His mouth twisted, derisively. 'I suggest you go and make yourself a strong cup of tea, you look as if you need it.'

It was only after he had turned abruptly on his heel and left her that she began to wonder why she should resent his assumptions so much. After all, she did love Gray so why should Alain Duval's opinion of her matter at all? Maddeningly, for some reason however, it did.

CHAPTER SIX

CLARE lingered for as long as was humanly possible in the small storage room in the hope that by the time she finally emerged and returned to Gray's room, Alain would have left.

For one ghastly moment she thought she had misjudged her timing as she heard muffled voices, but, to her relief, it was Danielle who greeted her as she re-entered the bedroom carrying a glass of water and Gray's pain-killing tablets. She placed them firmly in his hand, watching as he swallowed them, and only then did she give her attention to the girl.

Danielle was dressed in an elegant little suit, the blue of which, Clare guessed, had been cleverly chosen to give emphasis to the colour of her eyes. Over her arm she carried a matching coat and her hair was tucked up beneath a fur hat. The effect was startling and Clare thought wryly of her own limited wardrobe of basic essentials. A nurse's pay allowed for few luxuries, but then she hadn't exactly Danielle's need of such beautiful clothes.

'I'm taking the car into town.' Danielle pulled on her gloves. 'I still have some Christmas shopping to do before it's too late. I meant to do it in England but . . .' her voice faded and Clare caught the anxious look she shot in Gray's direction, but if he was aware of any tension it didn't show as he fumbled on the lovely rosewood table beside his bed for a sheet of paper.

'Good idea. I'd been having the same thoughts myself, but it's not going to be quite so easy now, is it?' Clare saw the slight twist to his mouth as he said it, but was more concerned with her own sense of shock as she realised that in fact she had completely forgotten that Christmas was only a few days away.

'I've made a list,' Gray was saying. 'Or at least I got Pierre to make it for me. Just a few items. Would you mind?'

'*Mais non*, of course not.' Danielle took it, scanned it briefly and dropped it into her bag. 'As long as you're prepared to accept my judgment over colours, that is.'

'I trust your judgment implicitly, except in the matter of the third item, against which you will find explicit instructions.'

'Yes, I noted it.' The girl smiled briefly in Clare's direction and nodded, leaving Clare with the vague feeling that some kind of conspiracy was going on which somehow involved her but which she would be best not to question. In any case her mind was too fully occupied.

'I don't know how I can have been so foolish as to let it happen, but I'd completely forgotten about Christmas until you reminded me. I haven't bought a thing.' Her hands rose expressively. 'I'd been promising myself that I'd do it all in one mad rush on my next day off, but somehow I just didn't get around to it.'

'That's hardly surprising, and the fault is entirely mine.'

'Oh no,' she began to protest, but Gray intervened.

'Oh yes. We fell into your life, Danielle and I, and took it over. We had no right and the very least we can do is to try and make amends.'

'There's really no need, and you didn't . . . take over my life as you put it.'

'No?' His brow rose and she saw the faint smile. 'Then that's a pity. Perhaps I must try harder.' Clare felt the colour in her cheeks and was glad he couldn't see it. 'In the meantime, of course you must take some time off.'

'But I can't possibly. I've only just arrived and I'm here to work.'

'That doesn't make you a prisoner.' For some reason she sensed a faint anger in his voice. 'You're a guest, in any case I don't need constant watching, Clare. For pity's sake don't start treating me like an invalid who has to be guarded day and night. I'd expected something different from you.'

The unexpected sharpness caught her off guard and for a moment she wondered just what he had expected from her. She forced her lips into a smile.

'Well, if you insist, actually I'd be glad of some time to go and buy a few things. It shouldn't take long.'

'Take as long as you need.' His hand moved to a drawer. 'You'll need some money.'

A denial hung on her lips as she realised how foolish it would be. Naturally she would be paid wages, though the amount hadn't been discussed and the amount he put on the table in francs now made her look up quickly. As if sensing her reaction he said, 'I know the amount there. Danielle arranged it for me so take it, buy yourself a dress or something to wear at Christmas as well.'

She took the proffered notes, but for some reason felt uneasy. It made everything seem so . . . so cold-blooded somehow, when all she wanted was to care for Gray, to see him get well again. As for a new dress. 'I don't suppose I shall have much occasion to dress up.' She said it lightly, unprepared for Danielle's response.

'Nonsense, of course you will. Gray is right, you are here as a guest, not simply to work. Besides,' her gaze scanned the plain uniform with a barely suppressed shudder, 'surely you cannot enjoy to be dressed so? You have a pretty face and a very attractive figure. Why hide it? Gray does not need a reminder that you are a nurse.'

'No. I'm sure he doesn't,' Clare murmured. She didn't add that somehow she thought Alain Duval might.

'So, it is settled then. You must come into town with me.'

'Oh but I can't, at least not immediately. I have to write up some notes for Dr Duval's visit tomorrow and he will want the information before he can begin the new tests.'

'Well then, in that case write your notes and meet me later. We will have lunch together and do your shopping afterwards. I will wait for you at Henri's.'

'Henri's?'

'*Oui*. It is where we shall have lunch. Pierre will drive you. Let him know what time you will be ready.'

Without waiting for Clare to answer Danielle bent to brush a kiss on Gray's cheek and with a wave of her hand was gone, leaving a trace of exquisite perfume behind.

Gray grinned. 'She's like a whirlwind, isn't she?'

'Yes she is rather, but then I seem to remember that she always was.'

'Not like you. You were always the quiet one.'

Her gaze flickered to his face, shyly. 'Was I? Yes I suppose so.'

'We must see what we can do to change that.' He frowned and held out his hand. 'Come here.'

She hesitated and he repeated it, sharply, his face suddenly white. 'For God's sake, must I speak to an open space, never knowing for sure if I'm even facing in the right direction?'

Cursing herself for her thoughtlessness she went to him and felt his fingers close over her own.

'That's better. You must stop hiding from me, Clare.'

'But I'm not.' It was true, she longed to be in his arms but, as Alain Duval had so arrogantly and truthfully pointed out, she was here to do a job. If she couldn't do that job she was going to be of no use to Gray and it would be better—for everyone, most of all for Gray—if she were to return home. She stared up at him, seeing the taut lines etched into his face. Would it be best if she left anyway, rather than perhaps have to discover that she would never be more to him than the child he remembered, the little mouse? Her lips quivered and, almost as if sensing something, he pulled her towards him.

'What is it, Clare? Something's wrong.'

'No,' she lied, quickly, feeling the tears prick at her lashes. His grip tightened and she saw the look of frustration as he tried to see her face.

'Don't lie to me, Clare, please. Whatever else you do, don't lie, I couldn't bear that. Don't you see, your word is all I have. I have to be able to rely on it.'

Clare gritted her teeth. 'Yes.'

'Then tell me.'

It wasn't so easy. She brushed a hand awkwardly through her hair. 'It's just that . . . well I was wondering if it's really such a good idea, my being here like this. I mean,' she groaned inwardly, 'I know Danielle and you . . . the house. It's too easy to forget . . . to forget that I'm here as a nurse, to do my job properly. I don't know that it's fair to you. I've been thinking that perhaps I should go back to England.'

His voice was bland as he held her. 'Are you telling me that that's what you want?'

She didn't answer. If only he would make things easier by agreeing with her—it would put an end to all the torment of being so near to him and yet so far.

'Is it?' he shook her.

'No, Gray, no, I . . .'

She heard his sharp intake of breath and felt herself being drawn towards him, then suddenly he was kissing her. There was only a split second's hesitation before she responded. This time she made no attempt to fight it. After all, it was what she wanted and what right had Alain Duval to try and rule her life? The mere thought of him made her respond more ardently than she might otherwise have done and she was aware of Gray's sudden tensing, as if she had taken him by surprise, and he moaned softly, drawing her even closer. It was some moments before they parted breathlessly and she was conscious of a slight feeling of guilt. This wasn't resolving her problem, it was making it worse and she moved restlessly.

'I don't want you to go, Clare. Now that I've found you I don't want to lose you again. You've become a sort of life-line to me. You were there just when I most needed someone.'

'But it could have been anyone,' she protested, only to be silenced by his fingers against her lips.

'It could, but it wasn't. It was almost as if fate had brought us together again. I need you, Clare, I want you. Don't desert me now, please.'

He wanted her, needed her. Her heart thudded uncomfortably. 'You're not giving me much choice, are you, Gray?'

He laughed, softly. 'I hope not. Say you'll stay.'

With the feel of his kiss still on her lips she nodded, her voice wavering into a whisper. 'Yes, I'll stay. I told you once before that as long as you need me I'll be here.' Despite Dr Alain Duval, she thought, rebelliously.

Reassured, Gray relaxed and after giving him his medication she left him listening to the radio and went to her room to write up the notes, adding to them the latest information which had come through from England. It took quite a while to bring it all up to date and by the time she had finished Gray was lying back in his chair with his eyes closed. Gently she persuaded him to eat a light lunch, then to rest for the afternoon.

'If you need anything just press the bell,' she reminded him. 'I shouldn't be away for long.'

'My dear girl, be as long as you please. I'm not going anywhere, after all.'

The slightly truculent note was back in his voice but she ignored it. It was only to be expected and though she hated to admit it, Alain was right, it would be too easy to pity Gray. By far the best thing any of them could do was to treat him as normally as possible.

As she got ready to meet Danielle she was grateful for Pierre Lescour's help. He was efficient and capable as many of the male nurses she had known and she felt no qualms about leaving Gray in his care for the few hours she would be away.

The car drove up, tyres crunching on the gravel drive, just as she ran down the steps. Dressed in a neat pair of trousers, boots and a bright cherry red jumper, she had crammed a matching woolly hat on her head and wore mittens on her hands. Not exactly chic, she thought wryly, but sensible. Not that she had had much choice, she just hoped it was right for Henri's.

To her relief she needn't have worried. Her eyes searched for Danielle as she entered the restaurant and she had already noted that the clientele were assorted, from obvious students to local business men and women and families with their children. Eating out was a family pastime in France. Food was something to be enjoyed and lingered over and she was no longer surprised to see even quite small children drinking watered-down wine with their meal.

Glancing at her watch she became aware of Danielle beckoning to her from a corner table and Clare slid gratefully into the seat beside her, smiling as she did so at the small mountain of beautifully wrapped packages.

'I take it you've had a successful morning,' she said.

'*Oui*, very successful.' Danielle produced a large bag. 'I bought this for Gray. What do you think?'

'I like it.' Clare admired a smart navy and white towelling robe. 'I'm sure he'll love it. Unfortunately I don't think my problem will be solved quite so easily. I haven't a clue what to give him myself.' And funds certainly wouldn't run to anything as expensive as the robe undoubtedly was.

The waiter produced the menu but Danielle dismissed it with a smile. 'We'll have the *moules mariniere* with lots and lots of crusty bread. Do you remember, Clare, how we enjoyed them so much when last you came to stay?'

'I do indeed.' Clare felt her mouth watering and when the large, steaming hot dish of mussels was placed on the table before them she ate hungrily, copying the method used by the French of somehow scooping up the mussel flesh, using the other shell to do so and drinking the juice.

Danielle sat back with a sigh of satisfaction. 'The French are not pretentious about their food. It is to be enjoyed and so is the wine.'

'I agree, though I'm beginning to think I've had a little too much.' Clare drained her glass and refused more of the dry, exquisitely flavoured muscadet. 'There's something very decadent about drinking during the day.'

'Ah, you think that because you are British. What is a meal without wine? You have too many inhibitions.'

'Well I'm glad to say we are gradually overcoming them.' She refused a dessert but sat contentedly while Danielle ate *tarte aux pommes Normande*, an open flan with beautifully arranged apple slices, with unashamed relish. They drank coffee and finally decided that it was time they did their shopping.

It had stopped snowing when they got outside but the sky was very grey and leaden. Danielle looked up at it wryly as they hurried, encumbered by parcels, to a large department store where she added the purchase of two silk scarves to her list. For Clare much of the enjoyment was simply in walking round and admiring the beautiful displays. She had still never become quite accustomed to the fact that even sweets were wrapped in attractive paper and decorated with ribbon, and she bought a box to give to Marguerite whose work load was bound to be increased with Christmas as well as an extra guest to feed.

For the rest of her gifts she had no idea what to choose. Gray seemingly had everything, except the one thing she couldn't give him, his sight. Danielle, without being aware of it, exuded an air of expense against which it was hard to compete and Clare had already resigned herself to the fact that it was better if she didn't even try.

Almost with a feeling of relief she finally managed to persuade her to return to the château, leaving her to complete the rest of her shopping alone.

'But are you sure you can manage?' Danielle asked.

'Of course. As a matter of fact I'd rather. There are one or two things I want to buy which I'd prefer to keep secret. Anyway I'll feel happier knowing you'll be there to keep Gray company.'

'Then, if you're sure you don't mind? I do seem to have rather a lot of parcels.'

Clare saw her safely installed in a taxi then returned to the task of completing her own list as quickly as possible. Despite Danielle's return she still felt guilty about leaving Gray.

Within an hour it was finished and she had also had a cup of coffee. She felt satisfied with her purchases. They may not have cost the earth but they were the best she could afford and a great deal of careful thought had gone into the buying of them. For Gray there was a new battery-driven razor so that he would be able to shave himself in the mornings. For Danielle a bottle of perfume, its fragrance light and flowery, for Pierre a small box of cigars. He wouldn't be expecting a gift but she wanted to thank him in some way for all the help he was giving. After that she had even found time to buy a new dress for herself. It hadn't been intentional, she had simply found herself staring up at the shop window admiring the soft, dusky pink dress which had somehow invited her to step in and buy it.

It was with a slight sense of shock that she came out into the street again to discover that it was getting quite dark and the sudden realisation that she still had to find her way back to the château filled her with a mild sense of panic. She scanned the street. There were no taxis and even had there been the cost would have been exorbitant. Enquiring about buses she was horrified to learn that there wouldn't be one along for at least another hour and even then she would need to walk some distance to the château.

She was standing unhappily on the pavement pondering what to do next when a large dark car slid to a halt in front of her. She gave it only a cursory glance, annoyed with herself for having been so foolish as not to ensure that she could get back safely. Perhaps if she telephoned they would send the car to fetch her, though the thought of having to do so and admit to her folly didn't appeal.

She was grudgingly accepting the fact that she had little alternative when the car's window purred down and a voice spoke her name.

'Miss Summers. Can I give you a lift?'

Oh no, it wasn't possible. Her heart sank as she looked into the enigmatic features of Alain Duval. Clutching the parcels which seemed suddenly determined to evade her grasp, knowing that her hair was windswept and her cheeks flushed by the cold, she remained rooted to the spot.

'No, thank you. I wouldn't dream of putting you to so much trouble. I'm waiting for the bus.'

The merest flicker of movement touched his lips. 'Then I'm afraid you're in for a very long wait. The last left over an hour ago.'

Aghast she stared at him. 'But it can't have.'

'I assure you it has. Of course there would normally be another, but heavy snow has blocked some of the roads. You may have noticed had you cared to look, that there isn't much traffic of any kind around.'

She had noticed, vaguely, but only now did the truth of what he had said fully register. The streets were almost deserted. As she stood debating wildly on some other method of reaching the château, anything rather than be forced to accept his offer of a lift, the car door opened and he was coming towards her. She stepped back involuntarily, and in so doing dropped her parcels. Before she could move he had retrieved them, his tall frame straightening up to an intimidating height, but to her chagrin he made no attempt to return them to her.

'I suggest you get in, unless you want us both to freeze to death.' He was holding the door open, waiting, his mouth a cynical line.

'I assure you I'm perfectly capable of walking, Doctor.'

A slight frown of impatience drew the dark brows together. 'I don't doubt it and I'd be quite capable of allowing you to do just that under any other circumstances.'

'What do you mean?'

'My concern is for my patient.' His tone was maddeningly cool. 'If I'd realised that you meant to absent yourself for any length of time, I would have made other arrangements. As it is, I suggest that the sooner you get back to your duties the better.' Even as he was speaking he had taken her by the arm and she found herself being propelled towards the car and into the passenger seat, then he was striding round to climb in beside her. He had already slipped the car into gear and they were moving effortlessly away before she found her voice and managed to steady it sufficiently to speak.

'I have not, as you put it, been out for any length of time, Doctor, merely a couple of hours in order to do some Christmas shopping, and my patient has not been neglected during that time. As a matter of fact he was sleeping and Pierre is perfectly capable . . .'

'I hardly see the relevance.' His tone stung her to silence. 'Are you or are you not here to do a job?'

Her teeth ground together in frustration. So they were back to that again. He was determined to make her feel inadequate. 'You know I am.'

'Then in that case I don't think anything more needs to be said. You can hardly do it if you are careless enough to get yourself stranded miles away from the château. As for walking back,' his gaze slid briefly from the mirror to her face and she was only too well aware of the familiar expression of contempt, 'I begin to get the impression that you go out of your way to invite trouble. Have you any idea how far it is? Did it even occur to you that it will be dark in less than half an hour?'

She sat in the luxurious seat, her hands locked together in angry frustration, made all the more intense because she knew he was partly right. Perhaps she had been wrong to leave Gray, even though he had been adequately cared for. Certainly she should have made sure she could get back in time, but how could she have known that the bus would fail to turn up?

'I promise you it won't happen again,' she said, stiffly. 'I won't leave the château in future without your permission.'

'Now you're being ridiculous.'

She was, and knew it, but her eyes widened angrily. 'But you just said . . .'

'I simply said that if you wish to go out, it is surely a wise precaution to ensure that you can get back, not that you should become a prisoner, Miss Summers.'

She clamped her mouth rigidly on a response,

staring out of the window rather than look at him. He really was the most objectionable man she had ever met, and the worst of it was that he had a habit of making her appear to be in the wrong.

The car ate up the miles and she found herself studying his hands as they rested effortlessly against the wheel, relaxed, yet always fully in control, just as he would be in control of anything he touched. The thought came from nowhere and for some ridiculous reason left her feeling shaky. What would it be like to be loved by a man like Alain Duval, she wondered. Was he capable of any human warmth and emotion, or did he see everything in terms of his job, with a clinical, whiter than white coldness?

She stared up at his profile. There was something about the sensuous mouth, the firm line of his jaw which made her doubt it, yet imagination seemed to send a fire rushing through her veins and she jerked upright in the seat. He turned, questioningly, to look at her as if expecting her to say something and she flushed, releasing her breath slowly as she imagined for one moment that he might actually have been able to read her thoughts.

'Go to sleep if you want to. There's nothing to see and we still have a way to go.'

What was the matter with her? Why on earth should a crazy thought like being kissed by him even enter her mind? It wasn't even as if she liked the man.

She leaned back, forcing herself to close her eyes as if she was obeying him. Her pulse was racing far too fast even to contemplate sleep, but the last thing she wanted was that he should realise the effect his presence was having on her.

CHAPTER SEVEN

CHRISTMAS had come and gone almost like an un-announced stranger before Clare was even really aware of it. They had all made an effort. One of the large trees from the estate was cut down and brought in to be decorated with baubles and tinsel and the presents were stacked beneath it. But it was, Clare realised, just that, an effort, an attempt to be cheerful.

On Christmas morning after breakfast they went to church and returned to open presents. She had exclaimed happily over Gray's gift to her, a soft blue sweater, and Danielle's which had been a small case fitted with beautiful cosmetics. She was well aware that both must have cost the earth and her own contributions, for all they were received with apparent pleasure, couldn't compete.

After a light lunch she walked with Gray along the snow-covered drive, and in the evening there was dinner, a veritable orgy of food and wine. The fact that Alain arrived, having obviously been invited to share it with them, and sat opposite her looking acutely masculine in a dark suit, his expression hidden behind the muted glow of the candles, turned the meal into an ordeal Clare would rather have avoided. And yet she knew she was being unreasonable. If anything, he was going out of his way to put her at her ease. He was even almost human.

'My name is Alain,' he corrected her softly as he handed her a glass of Calvados when the meal was over. 'Surely we don't have to observe the formalities, not at Christmas, Clare.'

For some reason the sound of her own name on his lips sent a tiny shiver of pleasure through her. She could even almost forget that she disliked him and then, with one sudden movement, he kissed her. It lasted only a few seconds, his lips descended upon hers and for a crazy moment she had experienced the heady sensation of floating through space, only to come to earth with a bump as he released her. Speechlessly she stared at him, willing her heart to resume its normal beat, then he gazed upwards and she followed his glance to the bunch of mistletoe and for some reason disappointment hit her like a wave.

'Shame to waste it,' he murmured with a hint of laughter in his eyes and she knew that her cheeks were scarlet with mortification.

For the rest of the evening she studiously avoided him. It wasn't difficult. Gray was gradually becoming bad-tempered and she purposely followed him when he got up and walked out of the room. In a way she had been expecting it. With each day now Gray was getting a little stronger, the leg was less painful and he was recovering well from the physical effects of the accident, yet, perversely, she found herself bearing the brunt of his temper which, as she was rapidly discovering, could be sharp to the point of being hurtful.

It was inevitable of course, she realised that, and consequently made allowances. As his strength gradually returned so he became more and more aware of the limitations placed upon him by his failing sight.

Walking quietly into the library she found him standing, brooding, at the window, staring out as if he might be able to refresh his memory of what was there, the things he had always taken so much for granted. She knew he was aware of her, though he made no attempt to turn as he said bitterly, 'It's getting worse. Even the shadows are getting darker and I'm scared, scared as hell. I'm almost completely blind.'

She stood, toying desperately with the idea of lying. It was getting worse, imperceptibly, but nonetheless there was a deterioration. Gradually even the shadows he saw now would be gone. She would have lied, she knew it then, if it had been any use. As it was he saved her from having to make the decision. He turned slowly and she was shocked to see the pallor of his face, the taut lines of fear, and instead of answering she went to him quickly and found herself enveloped in his arms, heard the quick intake of his breath almost like a sob as he said, 'Thank God I have you, Clare. I couldn't bear it without you.'

She held him in the circle of her arms, comforting him as she would have comforted a child, saying nothing until he was calmer.

'You mustn't give up hope. Alain still has to do more tests.'

'Tests. I'm sick of them. Why don't they just tell me the truth? Or perhaps I don't need to be told. Is that what they're waiting for, so that I can gradually realise it for myself and save them the job?'

'No,' she protested quickly. 'That isn't true.'

'Isn't it?'

'I wouldn't lie to you. I gave you my word, remember?'

'Oh yes, I remember, but how can I be sure?'

She bit her lip, ashamed because she so nearly had betrayed his trust, then a voice spoke quietly from the doorway. She wondered how long Alain had been standing there. 'You can believe her because she is telling you the truth, Gray.' Her gaze rose gratefully to him as he sauntered, hands in pockets, into the room. 'If there had been anything to tell, don't you think that I would have to come to you? Surely we've known each other long enough for that?'

'Then why are my eyes getting worse and why is nothing being done?'

Clare flinched at the bitterness in Gray's voice, but if Alain was aware of it he gave no sign. Quite the contrary, he appeared remarkably calm, almost too calm, she thought irritably.

'Something is being done, Gray. I would have told you tonight anyway and I suppose now is as good a time as any. I'm pretty certain now that I know what the problem is. No,' his hand rose, 'I'm not going to commit myself, but I've been studying the results of all the tests we've done so far and they all point in the right direction. I want you to come to the clinic in a few days time. I'll phone and let you know exactly when,' he looked at Clare and she realised she was still holding Gray's hand. 'I want to do a couple more tests and take another look at your eyes under certain conditions, which is why I want you to come to me rather than have it done here. I may even want you to stay overnight.'

'And will all this produce the answers or is it just another delaying tactic? If so I can do without it.'

'I think it will give me the answers, Gray. Trust me, trust Clare.'

She felt Gray's hand tighten over hers with a kind of possessiveness which made her wince.

'I do.'

'That's good.' For a long moment Alain's gaze lingered on her face, but she couldn't read the expression she saw there before he turned away.

'I'll call you when I have a room ready, and now I'd better go and say my goodbyes to Danielle.'

'You're leaving?' Clare felt an unreasoned sense of disappointment.'

'It's late and I'm on call tomorrow. In any case, I think you could do with some sleep yourself, Gray.'

He laughed, mirthlessly. 'I don't sleep.'

'In that case I'll leave you something. I have a few tablets with me. I rather thought they might be needed.' His gaze moved to Clare. 'I'll let you have them, Sister.'

She nodded, dumbly and followed him out. So it was back to the formalities again. Suddenly she wished she was back in England enjoying a normal Christmas without complications.

Three days later, as she was coming down the stairs in search of Marguerite, the telephone rang. Clare answered it automatically, a little frown of annoyance on her face as she tried to remember the list of things Gray had despatched her to attend to. She had the distinct impression of late that she had begun to take on the duties of secretary as well as nurse, and though she was only too pleased to see him taking an interest in things rather than sitting brooding, he didn't seem to understand or care that she couldn't simply drop everything to go chasing after Pierre with letters which he had begged her to write for him and which he now required posting.

It had taken most of the morning to persuade him to take his pills and to allow her to carry out the routine checks which were necessary in order that she could keep up the report which would be so vital when the final decision as to whether to operate or not, was made. Clare found it hard to keep her temper when she found herself put off as Gray made another and yet another telephone call, all to people obviously connected with his work.

'Surely the pills can wait for half an hour,' he insisted, roughly. 'I've just a few more calls to make, they're important.'

'So are the pills,' she had responded with unaccustomed anger, then shrugged, prepared to humour him. 'Well, I suppose they can wait, just for half an hour, but no more, mind.' Half an hour wouldn't really make any difference and it would probably do more harm than good to insist. But when that half an hour had passed and she had walked determinedly into his room, it was to find him still talking on the telephone.

She waited, quietly, so as not to disturb him and busied herself purposely, trying not to listen. The time gave her an opportunity to study him and she realised with a slight sense of shock that suddenly he seemed older. He *was* older than she was of course, but until now she had never really been aware of it. He was still good-looking but pain had etched fine lines into his features and there was a hardness about his mouth, almost as if it had set into a permanent line of resentment.

Idly stacking books which had been left on the floor, it was some moments before she suffered the embarrassing realisation that he was actually unaware of her presence. Looking back on it, she remembered that he hadn't lifted his head as he usually did when she came into the room, but she had assumed that was because he was talking. Only now, as she heard him laugh softly and the faint, answering ripple of a voice at the other end of the telephone, a woman's voice, did she realise her mistake.

Her hands tensed against the glass of water she held as she heard the soft inflection in his voice and saw the smile.

'My darling Francine, you're incorrigible. Of course I've missed you. How could I not?'

Feeling as if a cold hand had suddenly clutched at

her heart, Clare moved, turning instinctively to leave the room before he became aware of her, but the sound must have reached Gray and his head jerked up sharply.

'Who is it? For God's sake, can't I have any privacy?'

'I'm sorry.' She felt as if her feet were rooted to the spot. 'I didn't mean to intrude but I have my job to do. You did say half an hour and these pills must be taken—now.'

His hand waved vaguely in the direction of the table. 'Just leave them. I'll take them later.'

She steeled herself to go to him. 'No, I'm sorry, that won't do.' She was only too well aware of the caller on the other end of the telephone but her chin rose firmly. 'I have the pills here, Gray, and a glass of water.'

'Oh, for pity's sake.'

He snatched them from her. She pressed the glass into his hand and watched him swallow.

'There, satisfied, gaoler?'

The muscles of her throat tightened but some-how she managed to answer. 'Perfectly, thank you.' She turned to go, glad to escape, only to pause at the door as he called her name.

'Oh, by the way, would you get Pierre to take these to the village and post them later?'

She returned, taking the batch of envelopes from his hand. His attention was already back with the voice at the other end of the telephone and she experienced a pang of unreasoned jealousy. After all, Francine could be anyone, eighty years old, fellow artist, someone's wife. Instinct told Clare that she was none of those things and the knowledge hurt.

Closing the door behind her she paused for a moment. There was so much about Gray's life she didn't know, had no part in. He had said he needed her and when she was in his arms she knew that he wanted her. So why at this moment did she feel like a total stranger?

The voice spoke insistently in her ear, breaking into her reverie. 'Hullo, Clare, are you there?'

'Wh . . . oh yes. I'm here, Doctor. I was just putting a tray down before I dropped it. I have my hands rather full.'

There was an imperceptible silence from the other side and the tightness in her throat was like a physical ache. 'Is something wrong?'

'No.' The word was dragged from her. 'No of course not. Why should there be?'

'No reason. I must have imagined it.' The curtness was back in his voice. 'I just rang to say I have a room free in a couple of days and I'd like to get Gray in straight away so that I can start the new tests.'

'That's marvellous. He'll be glad things are moving at last.'

'Then let's hope they move in the right direction. I can't promise any miracles, Clare, you'd better make Gray realise that, and remember it yourself too.'

As if she of all people needed any reminder of what lay ahead. She was only too well aware of it and the possibility of Gray being blind haunted her, but she didn't need any reminder from Alain Duval to keep her personal feelings under control. 'Don't worry, Doctor, I'm not likely to forget.'

'Good. You'll accompany him to the clinic of course. I'll send my car.'

'Oh, but there's no need.'

'I think I'm capable of deciding what's necessary, Sister.'

Yes of course he was. She bit her lip. 'I'm sorry, Doctor.'

'I know how Gray feels about the whole business and I think he'll be less tense with familiar things around him. Besides which he'll be more comfortable.' There was a momentary pause, almost as if he expected her to fill it. 'I may want to keep him in. I did warn him. I don't want to dwell on it so if you just pack what you think he may need, just in case.'

'I'll see to it, Doctor.' Unconsciously her hand tightened against the 'phone. 'How soon after the tests . . .'

'Will I know if I can operate? About a week.' There was a silence during which she had the uncanny feeling that he could almost see her face. 'It'll soon pass and you'll have enough on your mind keeping Gray occupied. That will be your job and it's not going to be easy.'

'I don't expect it to be easy, Doctor,' she said sharply. 'I don't ask that it should be. The only thing I'm interested in is seeing Gray well again.' She slammed the telephone down and stood breathing hard. Realising what she had done she stared aghast at the instrument, half expecting it to ring again, but it didn't. Blast the man, she thought, picking up the tray and the bundle of letters and carrying them through to the kitchen. What was it about him that every time they came into contact it was like two live wires touching, and she was always the one who got burned?

It was with a certain amount of reluctance that she went back upstairs later and then she purposely avoided Gray's room, going instead straight to her own. It was difficult to judge between necessity and a desire to protect someone of whom one was very fond. She found herself staring at her reflection in the mirror as she unpinned the white cap and eased the band of tension which had been gathering all morning, by running her fingers through her hair. The chestnut curls framed her face softening her expression and with a sudden gesture of distaste she took the navy dress off and slipped into a pale blue woollen one which moulded gently to her figure. It was like looking at a different person and it wasn't only her appearance, she felt different. 'I'm not just a nurse,' she thought, with an edge of defiance, 'I'm a human being too, a woman, and I have feelings.' Feelings which at the moment were confused. Only a moment ago, without being consciously aware of it, she had thought of Gray as someone she was very fond of. Surely it should have been as the man she loved? She did love him and nothing would change that. He had been the centre of her world for too long, to let something . . . someone as vague and unreal as a woman called Francine change it. Or a man like Alain Duval. Now why had she thought that? Her hands pressed to her cheeks and her fingers brushed against her lips as if they could brush away the feel of those others pressed to hers, blot out the memory of the silent laughter in his eyes.

She turned as a tapping came at the door and, to her consternation, it was Gray who answered her call to enter.

'Gray, is something wrong?'

He held out his hand betraying his insecurity in a room with which he was unfamiliar. 'No, at least, not exactly.'

She went to him quickly. 'What do you mean? I'm sorry I didn't realise you had called me.' She had been so wrapped up in her own thoughts.

'I didn't. Don't feel so guilty.' He silenced her protest and she felt his fingers touch the soft fabric of her dress. 'I don't need anything except to talk to you.' He smiled and his features relaxed into those of the Gray she knew and remembered. 'You're not wearing your uniform. I'm glad. This makes you seem more real, more . . . reachable somehow.'

She held her breath as he drew her closer. Why should he want to reach her? That smile had been for Francine only a few minutes ago. Her laugh was forced. 'As a matter of fact I was just reminding myself that I'm a woman too. One tends to forget. It's the uniform.'

'I don't see why you need to wear one. It's not as if I'm in a hospital.'

'No, that's true, but I am a nurse. That's why I'm here.' She reminded him gently.

'And is that the only reason, Clare?'

'I . . . I don't know what you mean. Why else?'

'I don't know.' His hand was touching her hair. 'I'd sort of hoped that your reasons might be more personal. That perhaps it was because you cared for me.' His breathing quickened. 'Is that possible, Clare, my darling? It was just my imagination that led me to believe that you do feel something, for me?'

A lump seemed to have settled in her throat so that it was difficult to speak and when she tried suddenly there were tears in her eyes. 'Oh Gray.' She felt too confused. The answer should have been ready but somehow it wasn't. None of the past few days seemed real. It was like a dream from which she knew she must wake, but not before she knew what the ending would be.

His face was against her hair. 'I'm sorry about what happened.' His lips kissed her chin lightly, moving slowly, teasingly to her mouth where it became more ardent. She responded eagerly, conscious of a need to reinforce her own feelings in some way. 'I didn't mean to snap at you as I did,' he said, softly. 'It's just that I haven't got used to the idea of not knowing when someone else is in the room. You took me by surprise.'

Would it have mattered, she wondered, if he hadn't been talking to Francine? She thrust the thought away. 'It takes a bit of getting used to for me too. We've both got to make adjustments,

Gray, at least temporarily.'

'Dear Clare,' his mouth tightened, 'ever tactful. You won't even admit the possibility that I might never see again, will you?'

'No, because I don't give up hope and neither must you. As it happens I was going to come and see you, to tell you . . . Alain called. He has a room. He wants you to go in to the clinic.'

His expression froze. 'When?'

'In two days.' Seeing the sudden anguish in his face she wanted to comfort him but he made no attempt to take her in his arms again. Instead he turned away but she knew without being told that he was afraid. 'Alain is sending the car.' Unthinkingly she touched his arm and suddenly, with a ferocity which shook her he had gripped her arms and was clinging to her, kissing her again, this time with an intensity which was frightening. It was almost as if he was afraid he would lose her if he let go. But he wouldn't, she would see to that. Rocking him gently in her arms she knew that for as long as he needed her, she would wait. For ever if need be.

CHAPTER EIGHT

THE car arrived and they drove in virtual silence to the clinic. Somewhat to Clare's surprise, Danielle had insisted on accompanying them. At first she had made light attempts at chatter but, to her relief, and she was sure, to Gray's, these had faded after a while and she had stared instead out of the window, leaving Gray to a mood of moroseness which Clare had known better than to try to rouse him from. He was edgy, predictably, but she coped with it, knowing the reasons. Gray wouldn't admit his fear but it was there all the same.

As they drew up at last outside the Duval clinic, wheels crunching in the snow, Clare found herself staring up at the building in some surprise. She wasn't sure what she had expected but it certainly wasn't this beautifully modern, light airy building in whose windows, trees and snow-covered slopes were reflected.

Stepping out of the car the air bit so icily that her breath fanned white in front of her and she shivered. Gray was pale but he smiled as Alain came down the steps towards them, ushering them through the glass doors and into the warmth.

His gaze passed briefly over Clare. At Gray's insistence she had discarded her uniform in favour of a chunky sweater and skirt, topped by a high-collared coat. She thought she detected a faint note of disapproval but there was no time to dwell on it as, with grudging admiration, she watched him getting his patient settled with the minimum of fuss. Almost before Gray was aware of it he was being shown to a room which, though not large was both pretty and attractively furnished. Her eye mentally noted the matching curtains and bedspread in a warm shade of pink which made the snow beyond the windows seem almost unreal. Apart from the bed there was a table and comfortable chair, a telephone and a television set for patients who were recovering from operations and wished to use it. For those who didn't there was a radio.

It was luxury compared to the wards at St Mary's, and it wasn't in any way exceptional for, as they had walked along the corridors she had seen that each room, though some in different colours, was basically the same.

She found herself looking at Alain, wondering if he was responsible for the design and careful thought which must have gone into this clinic. She wished she knew more about the kind of man he really was. But why should she assume there was some mystery, simply because she didn't know all there was to know. She had the feeling that there was a side to this man which no-one ever reached.

Having seen Gray settled Clare said her good-byes, leaving Danielle to linger and meet her later in the reception hall.

Alain followed her out and came to a halt beside her in the corridor.

'When are you going to make a start on the tests?'

'Straight away. There's no reason to wait. The sooner we get it over with the better.'

She nodded glancing at her watch. 'There's not much point in my hanging around pacing up and down.'

'None at all. You'd only get in the way and my staff have enough to do without having to answer constant queries from anxious visitors. I suggest you go back to the château, I can always call you when there's any news. I imagine you'll be waiting by the 'phone.'

His tone was harsh, almost as if he was angry though she couldn't imagine why, unless he simply wanted her out of his way. She shook her head.

'No, if there's any chance at all that Gray can go home tonight I want to be here. He'll only brood if he has to stay any longer than is absolutely necessary.'

'That's entirely up to you.' She felt the tension as his eyes raked her scornfully. 'I'm sure you'll be able to keep his mind off things.'

She recoiled, sensing that he was deliberately taunting her again and deliberately she forced her gaze to meet his. 'I hope so, Doctor. At least you can be sure I'll try.'

Anger blazed in the satanic eyes as they searched her face and she steeled herself for something, not quite knowing what, but it didn't come. Instead he simply turned on his heel and walked away from her, leaving her to stand in the corridor feeling as if she had been hit by a tidal wave. Turning away she began to walk towards the exit. Seconds later she heard the door of his office slam to a close.

Danielle ordered coffee and they sat in silence until it arrived, neither of them caring to give voice to their doubts or hopes.

When the cups were set before them, Danielle spooned sugar into hers, staring at the circling froth of cream. 'This is almost like old times,' she said, dully, 'except that I don't feel it will ever be quite the same again.'

Clare had to resist the urge to keep looking at her watch, but her gaze seemed to be drawn inexorably to the church in the square opposite the café where they sat, and the hands of the clock seemed scarcely to move at all.

'Gray is going to be all right.' She shook her head, refusing the proffered cigarette. 'Dr Duval is good at his job. If anyone can make Gray well I'm sure he can.'

Danielle sipped at her coffee, studying Clare over the rim of the cup. 'You don't like Alain, do you? I don't know why but you two seem to strike sparks off each other, or is it perhaps the attraction of opposites?'

Clare raised her own cup to her lips and drank the scalding coffee too quickly. 'I really don't think about him one way or another. I'm not interested except in his skills as a doctor, that's all that matters. As for attraction,' she laughed unsteadily, 'I don't know where you get that idea from. I'm afraid the good doctor isn't my type. He's too arrogant to start with, always has to be right, and the damnable thing is, he usually is.' She ground another cube of sugar angrily into her cup.

'I suppose he does give that impression, to someone who doesn't really know him. It's a pity because Alain wasn't always as you see him now. It seemed to happen quite suddenly. I suppose the death of his wife had a great deal to do with it.'

Clare felt a sudden tingling sensation spread over her scalp. 'His wife?'

'Yes,' Danielle's eyes widened. 'Oh, but of course you wouldn't know. He and Hélène had been married for only two years when she was killed in an air crash. It was very tragic. She had been visiting her grandmother who had had a heart attack. The old lady was recovering and Hélène felt it was safe to leave her, but on the way home . . .' Her hands rose, sadly expressive. 'Since it happened Alain has been . . . how do you say, withdrawn. Now his work is everything to him, almost as if he is afraid to let anyone come close to him again in case he might be hurt. I know how he must feel. We all loved Hélène, but it isn't good. He is too young to throw himself away.'

The realisation that he had actually been married shook Clare. She had accused him, the words came flooding back now, of having no feelings, of being cold and utterly ruthless, and it was absolutely true, yet suddenly she felt an overwhelming sense of pity for the agony he must have suffered which had made him the way he was. Her throat tightened.

'I had no idea.' She stared out of the window but saw nothing. And if she had known, would it have made any difference? She shook the thought away quickly, afraid to let it develop. What was the point? He had made it perfectly clear that their relationship was strictly that of doctor and nurse and even if it wasn't, it was Gray she loved, Gray who needed her.

Having drunk their coffee they passed the next few hours desultorily shopping, anything rather than just sit and think about Gray and what was at stake. Only as the afternoon wore on did Clare finally allow herself to look at her watch.

'I think I'd better get back to the clinic. The tests should be over by now unless anything unforeseen has cropped up.' She pressed Danielle's arm. 'With any luck I'll bring him back to the château tonight. If not, well, I'll see you later.'

'Alain will send you home in the car.'

'I'd rather he didn't.'

'But it's all arranged. He told me before we left the clinic.'

Oh did he indeed, Clare thought, hotly. Obviously he was taking no chances of her missing her bus again.

They parted company at the clinic. She waited briefly as Danielle was driven away by Henri who had had the car waiting, then she made her way slowly, almost reluctantly, up the steps and in through the glass swing doors. With her hands sunk in her pockets and her head lowered she walked quickly past Alain's office, grateful that the door remained firmly closed. To meet him now would be to rouse too many conflicting emotions. Her one concern must be for Gray. There might be some news, however slight.

Outside his room she paused, dreading the moment when she must go in. She must steel herself to expect nothing, for Gray's sake she musn't let him see that she was worried sick.

There was a smile on her lips as she walked into the room. It faded as she saw that he wasn't alone but had a visitor, a woman, a beautiful woman who turned questioningly in her direction giving Clare a heart-stopping vision of elegance as her gaze took in the blonde hair and the green eyes which studied her with a hint of bored amusement now.

Conscious of her own windswept state and lack of make-up, Clare tugged at her gloves as she moved towards the bed. 'I'm sorry, forgive me, I didn't realise anyone would be here.' Did she imagine the look of uneasiness in Gray's eyes? He sounded in remarkably high spirits.

'Clare, don't run away. Come here.' He held out his hand, waiting.

The tests must have gone well, she thought with relief, or was his good mood more to do with the presence of the visitor? 'I'm glad you're back, I want you to meet someone, Clare this is Francine, Francine, Clare, a good friend of mine.'

She felt a tightening in her chest. So this was Francine. She should have known that it would take someone exceptional to produce the effect she had seen so clearly on Gray's face that day. Her lips formed a smile as an elegant, bejewelled hand reached out languidly to meet hers. The scarlet mouth smiled.

'But of course, I guessed. Your description was perfect, Gray darling. She is just as you said.'

As the cool gaze scrutinised her Clare wondered just what Gray's description of her had been. Whatever it was Francine's interest was superficial. She had already returned to Gray and Clare felt as if she had been summarily dismissed as the two laughed together. Watching Gray she hadn't seen him so excited or so animated before and it was obvious that it was the woman who was responsible for it. Clare tore her gaze away. She couldn't blame him, but the thought filled her with depression as she turned away, knowing that they were oblivious to her presence.

'But Gray, darling, you must,' Francine's voice pleaded. 'How can you disappoint so many people, your friends so? How can you disappoint me?' The beautiful lips pouted. 'I am counting on you, you know that.'

'I don't think you should. I told you not to.'

Clare saw the tautness of his mouth and wanted to intervene but something held her back. It was as if she was rooted to the spot, didn't even exist.

'Nonsense. All I need is the word and I shall arrange it all. You can leave everything to me. I shall put on an exhibition of your work in three months and I insist that you complete the portrait of me so that it can have pride of place. You promised, Gray. No, no, I won't listen to any excuses.'

In spite of her determination not to intrude Clare felt herself propelled forward by a surge of anger. Didn't this woman realise what she was saying?

'I really think that Gr . . . Mr Masterson should get some rest now. He's had a very long and tiring day and it is important that he gets a proper amount of sleep.'

The green eyes were like daggers of ice regarding her coldly, yet the voice was soft, with a hint of amusement, for Gray's benefit, Clare thought.

'But yes, it is thoughtless of me and you are right to remind me, Nurse.' The elegant figure rose slowly. 'How very efficient you are.' And how dull, the words seemed to imply, but Clare let them pass as she walked rigidly to the door to open it. She averted her eyes purposely as Francine bent to kiss Gray, lingering until Clare wanted to jerk her away from him.

Breathing deeply she waited until the door had closed behind Francine before forcing herself to speak bluntly. It wasn't something she wanted to say but for Gray's sake she must. In the corridor she turned to face her.

'*Au revoir*, Nurse Summers. It has been most interesting.'

'Madame, wait please, there is something I have to say.' She heard the quick sigh of impatience but wasn't going to be dismissed so easily.

'Are you not satisfied,' Francine drawled, pulling on her gloves. 'You have driven me away from

Gray when he was happy to have someone to cheer him a little, surely there can be nothing else.'

'It is about Gray that I must speak to you.' Clare forced herself to meet the intimidating gaze directly. 'I assure you I have no wish to deprive him of your company . . .'

'*Non?*' The scarlet mouth curved in silent laughter. 'I think perhaps you are lying, Miss Summers, that you are a little jealous.'

The colour drained from Clare's cheeks. 'My private feelings have nothing whatsoever to do with this.' Was that entirely true? She was jealous, but it was for Gray that she was concerned. 'I simply want to warn you, to advise you that it is unwise, perhaps even cruel, to speak to him about the possibility of putting on an exhibition of his work and certainly of his painting again.' She knew she was breathing hard and wished those eyes weren't fixed on her with such intensity. 'Perhaps you aren't aware that these tests Gray has been undergoing are being done in order to help Dr Duval decide whether an operation may help to restore Gray's sight and that even if he does operate, there is still a chance it may not be successful.'

For a moment there was silence, then, with a sense of shock she heard the soft ripple of laughter. 'My dear Miss Summers, how conscientious you are. I am sure you are quite expert at your job, how could you not be.' Clare felt herself subjected to a cold scrutiny from head to toe. 'But there is one thing you forget. I know Gray, know him very well, and I think I am perhaps best able to judge what he is capable of, which is certainly more than you appear to give him credit for, but then, you are after all, only his nurse, isn't that so?'

Before Clare could even begin to frame a reply Francine had turned on her elegant heels and walked away without a backward glance, leaving Clare feeling both sick and stunned. The words had been coldly calculated to have the maximum effect and had succeeded perfectly as Clare found herself wondering with a sinking feeling just how well Francine knew Gray.

CHAPTER NINE

IT seemed, to Clare, that Gray's return to the château brought with it a return to the ill moods he had suffered prior to his visit to the clinic, and she found it increasingly difficult to deal with them as the days went on. The reason was simple enough, being able to do something about it wasn't quite so easy. There had been no word from the clinic. She had considered telephoning and then discarded the idea. When there was any news Alain would be in touch. Until then they must all be patient but the burden still fell heaviest on Gray and for the first time she was aware of how little she could actually do to relieve it for him.

His nervousness showed itself in the way he snapped at her as she tried to make him more comfortable. She tried lessening her duties as much as it was humanly possible to do so in order to spare him the constant reminders of what was at stake, but even so there were some things which had to be done and she had to steel herself to go to his room now.

He was sitting close to the fire but shivering as if no amount of heat could warm him and her immediate instinct was to go to him and put her arms around him. Instead she put the tray with the pain-killing tablets and the eye drops which had been prescribed after the tests, onto the table, remembering to say something so that he would know she was there.

'Time for your drops, Gray.'

His head jerked up in her direction. 'You don't have to remind me. As if I could forget when you creep in and out every few hours.' He held his head in his hands. 'Why the hell don't you leave me alone, after all, it's not going to make any difference, so why fool ourselves?'

Clare bit her lip. It was becoming more and more difficult to deal with his bitterness, and even her silence was wrong.

'Don't sulk,' he snapped. 'I can't bear it when you go quiet on me. Fight back or do something. Anything, tell me I'm a bastard for treating you the way I do.'

'Will it make you feel any better?' she challenged with forced brightness only to recoil as his hand was flung up sending the glass of water she was holding, crashing from the tray, spilling over her uniform and sending the tablets rolling across the carpet. His face was ravaged with anger.

'No, it won't make me feel any better, but it relieves my feelings, makes me feel as if I can bend the bars of this . . . this prison even if I can't escape.'

Appalled by the stricken whiteness of his face Clare bent quickly with a stifled sob to retrieve the tablets. She knew that what was happening was perfectly natural. She had seen patients lash out like this before, it was a form of self defence, they had to hit out at something, but she had never before felt quite so helpless. It was as if there was a barrier suddenly between herself and Gray and it was of his own making, almost as if he didn't want her to be able to reach him. Tears welled up in her eyes, scalding and blinding, so that he was only a blur but even as she flinched, drawing back, she saw him turn, flinging out his hand.

'Clare, wait, I'm sorry, I didn't mean . . .' His voice was rough as he tried to reach her hand but even as she made to go to him the door opened.

'Gray, Gray darling.'

Clare couldn't watch. Feeling sick she let her hand fall and kneeling scooped up the tablets and the tray and got to her feet to find Francine regarding her with unveiled amusement. 'Nurse Summers, I hope you're not going to scold me again. I came to cheer Gray up. He looks as if he needs it. What have you two been doing, fighting?'

'There was a little accident, that's all.' Clare's glance went hotly from the beautiful face to Gray's. The change in him was staggering. All the anger had melted away and he was actually smiling. 'If you'll excuse me,' she murmured thickly. Taking two more tablets from the bottle and pouring fresh water from the carafe she held it out to Gray. 'Just take these please, then I'll leave you alone. I have quite a lot of work to do.' As he took them his hand briefly touched her own and she saw a look of . . . was it regret or impatience in his eyes. She didn't want to see. 'I have to write up a report.' It wasn't true but somehow she had to get out of the room and was conscious as she did so that Francine was watching.

Once outside the room she stood breathing hard against the door. It was some seconds before she realised that, with her hands full, she probably hadn't closed it properly because Gray's muffled voice came to her. As to why it should be muffled, only one reason occurred to her, he was undoubtedly in Francine's arms.

'I feel as if I'm a prisoner in my own house, as if I'm being suffocated. Can you understand that? Dear God, will it ever end?'

'But of course I understand, darling.'

Clare didn't wait to hear the rest. She fled to her room and grabbed her coat, shrugging herself into it as she ran. Gray wasn't the only one to feel suffocated. It was ironic that, although perhaps not in the same way, she was every bit as much a prisoner as Gray, held by her love for him and his need of her, but at least she was able to get away, if only temporarily.

She didn't even stop to think which direction she was taking. It didn't matter as long as she put some distance between herself and the château, anywhere, just so long as she had time to think and be alone for a while.

It had stopped snowing but a light covering lay on the drive and her shoes squeaked over it as she ran, head down, her eyes blurred by tears. It was bitterly cold but the fresh air might clear her head. She wasn't even conscious of the car drawing to a halt or the figure behind the wheel, sitting for a few seconds before getting out of his seat to bring her flight to a halt as she ran, literally, into his arms.

'Hey now, where are you off to in such a hurry?'

She stared bleakly up into Alain Duval's face, and to her chagrin she knew there were tears on her cheeks. Her mouth felt stiff from the effort not to give way to all the emotions which seemed to be pounding away at her but suddenly it was too much. She stifled a sob. Alain frowned, then without a word he ignored her protests and thrust her swiftly into the warmth of the car and got in beside her.

'Would you mind telling me what all this is about?'

Wiping the tears away with a gloved hand, Clare purposely avoided his gaze yet had the uncomfortable feeling that he could see right into her soul.

'I don't know what you mean. I was just out for a breath of fresh air.'

'Of course you were.' He said it with an infuriating calm. 'The fact that it happens to be below freezing and that you just happen to be in tears has nothing at all to do with it, I suppose?' His mouth tightened. 'What kind of a fool do you take me for, Clare? I'd like to know the cause.'

Incredulously she felt his hand brush lightly against her cheek, wiping away the wetness. The gesture was so unexpectedly gentle that she could only stare at him, feeling as if her limbs had turned to water. He was feeling sorry for her and she couldn't bear it.

'I really don't see that it's any business of yours.'

She hated the sound of the sharpness in her own voice.

'Are you quite sure of that?'

'Perfectly.' She moved imperceptibly away. 'My personal life has nothing whatsoever to do with you.'

'In this case,' the grey eyes narrowed, quizzically, 'I think it has. I warned you about the dangers of allowing yourself to become emotionally involved. That's what's happened, isn't it?'

She tried to turn away but, infuriatingly, he forced her to look at him and she was conscious of the sudden tautness of his jaw, the pulse working in his throat. 'No.'

'Are you in love with Gray.'

Her breath caught in her throat. She had never faced the question outright before and now that it had come, for some reason the words stuck in her throat. Maddeningly he seemed to take her silence for confirmation.

'I see,' his tone was scornful. 'And Gray, is he in love with you? He'd be a fool if he isn't.'

She choked on an answer as colour scalded into her cheeks. 'What right have you to ask questions like that, or to make such assumptions? Why don't you just leave me alone?'

'It's simple enough to answer.'

Blindly she pulled away from him, trembling, though whether from anger or because he was so close she couldn't tell. 'I . . . he needs me.'

'Ah, I see, and so you're going to become a martyr in his cause, is that it?'

Anger made her try to jerk herself free of his grasp. 'How dare you question my motives? Who are you to judge? Simply because you are so devoid of human feeling, must you reduce everyone else to the same level?'

She had gone too far and knew it as she saw the blaze of anger which whitened his face, but she was totally unprepared for the speed of his next action. Before she could even try to withdraw the words he had pulled her roughly towards him, holding her in a vice-like grip as his mouth came down ruthlessly upon hers. She felt as if the breath was being driven from her lungs. She hated him but there was no escape. Mercilessly his grip only tightened the more she fought and the pressure of his mouth increased until her head was reeling with sensations she had never imagined possible. It was as if a fire was coursing through her body, draining her strength and the will to fight. With a sob she submitted, her body relaxing against his, feeling the muscular hardness of his arms around her. Suddenly she didn't want to escape, wanted it to go on for ever. Her mouth turned hungrily up to meet his and she heard him groan, then she felt herself released so abruptly that she fell back, dazed, until he forced her chin up and said, mockingly. 'You're still a child, Clare, a child playing adult games. Well, take care, you might get hurt and so might other people.'

Before she could recover her breath he had leaned across her and flung the car door open. Feeling sick she staggered out and stood watching as he drove away leaving tyre marks in the snow.

Her hand went to her lips where she could still feel the pressure of his own upon them and she was shaken to discover that, far from being distasteful, she had actually enjoyed the sensation.

Furiously she dug her hands into her pockets and began to walk, striding out as if by so doing she could outpace her own confused emotions but by the time she returned to the château she felt even more confused than before.

It was dark when she did eventually get back and the lights were on as she went to her room to take off her coat before going to see Gray. She did so with a certain amount of reluctance which was only overcome by telling herself that it was pointless to try to avoid him and Francine. The sooner they were confronted the better.

Clare almost regretted the decision however as she entered the room to find Francine gathering up her bag and the gorgeous fur she had been wearing, and slipping her hand with a certain air of possession through Gray's arm.

'Come along, darling, or we shall be late.'

Clare came to a halt in the doorway, staring at Gray. 'But . . . surely you aren't going out? You know that Dr Duval left strict orders that you were to rest. You know you're going to need all your strength if the operation goes ahead.'

'Oh really, Nurse, aren't you being a little over-protective?' Francine glared at her. 'You treat Gray as if he were a child, but he is not.'

'I treat Gray as my patient, Madame, which he is. I want only what is best for him . . .'

'How very noble.' Her laughter held a subtly acid note. 'But are you sure? Or do you want what is best for yourself? If so, I warn you, Miss Summers, you cannot keep Gray here for ever.'

Clare gasped. 'I don't know what you mean.'

'I think you do.'

'Look, for pity's sake, can we cut out the arguments.' It was Gray himself who intervened. 'I'm going out, Clare, so just spare me the objections. Francine has been doing a lot of work towards putting on an exhibition for me. All I intend is that we go to the hall where she can describe the lay-out to me. That's all, I give you my word.' He was looking directly at her and she found the plea in his eyes disconcerting, but wasn't she right to object? With a hint of annoyance she found herself even beginning to question her own motives. Perhaps she was being over-protective, but the order had been Alain's.

Francine's hand was on Gray's arm and it tightened now, perceptibly, as she turned to Clare. 'You are being very foolish. Do you imagine I haven't already spoken with your precious Doctor? I assure you, we have his blessing.'

Clare flushed. If only they had made that clear in the first place, they might all have been saved a certain amount of unpleasantness, but she had the feeling that Francine had purposely withheld the information. 'Then in that case of course it's all right.'

'*Bon*, then we may go.' Her gaze flickered icily over Clare before she relinquished her hold on Gray's arm and walked to the door. 'I will check that the car is ready and wait for you downstairs, darling.' She swept away in a mist of exotic perfume which Clare found heavy and cloying.

She stood motionless as Gray picked up his coat, then paused. 'You worry too much, Clare. Please, don't, I'm perfectly all right.'

'Yes, of course you are.' She answered brightly, almost too brightly and he bent to kiss her lightly on the lips.

'You're adorable you know that? I don't know what I'd do without you to fuss over me, but don't let Francine get to you. This is strictly business I promise you.' He opened the door. 'Put your feet up, have a gin and tonic, or is lemonade more in your line?'

He was gone, leaving Clare staring dully after him feeling an odd stab of pain in her chest. Gray had spoken to her as if she was still the adolescent she had been when he had first seen her and the knowledge that, beside a woman like Francine, she must indeed appear very gauche and dull left her feeling incredibly depressed. Even more so as Alain's words kept ringing mockingly inside her head. 'A child playing adult games,' he had said. Just what did she have to do to prove that she was a woman and why all of a sudden, did she feel that it was necessary?

She decided after all to take Gray's advice. There was no point in moping and she had no intention of sitting around so that it looked as if she had deliberately been waiting for their return. In any case she would be glad of an early night.

Having showered she slipped a robe on over her nightie and went downstairs to the lounge. There was a huge fire burning in the hearth and having helped herself to a drink, a large gin and tonic, almost as if in defiance, she carried it to the sofa and sat in semi-darkness staring into the flames.

It was all a far cry from St Mary's and distance had an uncanny way of making familiar things desirable. Right now she would give anything to be back on her old ward, aching feet, the pressures of trying to fit too many jobs into too few hours and all. Anything to get away from the confusing tangle her life seemed to have become. Yet exactly what was it that she wanted to escape from?

An involuntary sigh broke from her lips, dying as the door bell rang insistently. After a while, since no one else had apparently made an attempt to answer it, she remembered that it was Marguerite's night off and got up reluctantly, conscious of the robe she wore swathed about her and her hair, dishevelled and still damp from the shower. With a vague frown of annoyance she wondered who on earth was calling at this hour, just when she had been planning on taking herself off to bed for that early night.

She held the door half open, peering into the darkness and the sight of Alain, standing on the steps, looking devastatingly handsome and for all the world as if he made a habit of calling at such an hour, seemed to rob her of her powers of speech, until she realised that he was scrutinising her state of undress with quiet amusement. Instinctively she drew the belt more tightly round her waist, unaware that it emphasised even more the slender curves, and wishing that she had at least taken the time to apply a trace of lipstick.

'I seem to have called at an awkward moment.' His voice held a note of laughter and only willpower kept her from closing the door and leaving him standing on the steps.

'I . . . no, not really, it's just that I was going to have an early night. I wasn't expecting visitors.'

'So I see.'

Her hand tightened on the door. 'Danielle is out, and so is Gray, but of course you know that . . .'

'I didn't come to speak to Danielle or to Gray. As a matter of fact I came to talk to you.'

'To me?' Her voice trembled.

'Why not?' He frowned. 'Look, is it really necessary to keep me standing on the doorstep. It's freezing out here.'

She would have liked to keep him permanently there but instead found herself reluctantly opening the door wider and leading the way to the lounge. His glance went briefly to the half-empty glass of gin and tonic and she had to resist the desire to insist that it was her first and only drink. Why was it that she was always on the defensive when he was around? She stood waiting.

'You said you wanted to talk to me.'

'Yes, that's right, I do.' He was studying the furnishings with interest. 'But not here.' He glanced at his watch. 'I'm going out for a meal. I don't suppose you've eaten, girls today seem to live on fresh air.'

As it happened she hadn't eaten, her appetite seemed to have vanished of late and not even the sight of the beautiful omelette, so carefully prepared by Marguerite had been able to restore it, until now, when, maddeningly, the mere thought of food made her stomach react noisily.

'I thought as much.' Infuriatingly he interpreted her silence as an acknowledgment. 'In that case I suggest you go and get dressed and join me. I'll give you ten minutes.'

Her lips parted on an angry protest. He just couldn't get out of the habit of ordering her life. 'I'm really not very hungry,' she lied.

'Nonsense. You have to eat. Besides, feeding you isn't exactly my prime concern, Sister. I have to confess, since you push me to it, that I have an ulterior motive. I want to discuss my patient and I don't particularly want to do it here, so be a good girl and hurry up.'

He stood implacably as a variety of expressions flickered across her face, including defiance, but she knew he had won. If it came to it she hadn't even a real excuse for refusing. The early night had merely been an escape from boredom, she was hungry and if he wanted to discuss Gray then it was her duty to do as he wished.

'It will take me a few minutes to slip into a dress and make myself presentable.'

'I should think a few seconds would be more than

enough.' His gaze slid over her slender figure and she had the unnerving feeling of being stripped naked before she fled to her room and dressed without any real thought as to whether the clothes she was throwing on were suitable. Her image, reflected in the glass gave no real assurance either. Her face was pale as she added a trace of lipstick to her mouth and flicked a comb through her hair. The dress, a pale blue-green, suited her, or at least she had always thought so until now. Whether it would be right for the kind of place they were going to was another matter. But then, she hadn't exactly had time to prepare and this wasn't meant to be a social outing, he had made it clear that it would be strictly business.

He had helped himself to a drink when she re-entered the room. Foolishly, she found herself looking for some hint of approval but the dark eyes betrayed nothing as he put down his glass and came towards her, taking her coat and helping her into it. His hand brushed against the nape of her neck, sending a shock wave running along her spine.

'Shall we go? I booked a table and they won't keep it for ever.'

He had been so certain she would accept his invitation then, she thought, with a certain amount of irritation as he ushered her out to the car, or rather, that she would obey his order.

She settled into the hugging luxury of the seat. 'Where are we going? I still don't see that it was necessary to drag me out in order to discuss Gray's progress.'

His eyes didn't leave the road as the car purred effortlessly along with flakes of snow darting like moths against the headlights. 'I didn't drag you.'

'No, but you didn't exactly give me a choice.'

'I didn't notice that you argued, Clare.' His glance flickered briefly in her direction and she sensed rather than saw the quiet amusement tugging at his mouth.

It was maddening the effect he seemed to have on her, the way he had of making her unsure of herself. No, she hadn't refused to come with him because she had had the uneasy feeling that if she had done so he was perfectly capable of doing just that, dragging her to the car by force if he felt like it. Alain Duval was a man who liked his own way and got it whether by subtle threats or other means, she didn't feel he would have too much conscience about it. But lurking at the back of her mind was also the tiny feeling of guilt that she had actually wanted to come.

It was ridiculous. She sat upright, her hands clenched. 'It still doesn't explain why we couldn't have talked at the château.'

'I told you, I haven't eaten, neither have you, and I don't like wasting time. We can kill two birds with one stone this way so why not just relax and enjoy it? The restaurant is nothing pretentious but the food is good and so is the wine. Better still, we can talk without having to shout to make ourselves heard.'

It all sounded very cosy. He had an answer for everything so she clamped her mouth on any response. She hated admitting defeat but had the distinct feeling that she would always be the loser in any battle of strength with this man.

At least he was right about the restaurant. It was pleasant, the sort of place she would have enjoyed coming to under different circumstances. It was crowded too, but she scarcely noticed the faces as they were led to a table. She was conscious of nothing but the hand firm under her elbow, almost as if he was afraid she might try to run away.

When they were seated he ordered drinks making no attempt to consult her as to her tastes or preferences. When it came she raised the glass to her lips prepared to dislike it and was pleasantly surprised. For some reason the knowledge angered her and she put the glass down sharply, spilling a little.

'Don't you like it? Would you rather have something else?'

'No, this is fine.' She frowned impatiently. Why on earth had she come? Merely sitting at a table in such close proximity to him, seeing the dark hair and those eyes was having a crazy effect on her, one she didn't like. The room was too hot, too noisy. Her hand gripped the small evening bag she had brought with her as her gaze searched for the exit.

'I'll order then we can talk.' Almost as if he had sensed her intention his voice cut sharply across her thoughts. 'After all, that's why we're here, isn't it?'

Yes it was, she thought, dully, and felt suddenly depressed. Watching the blur of his features above the glow of the candle as he studied the menu, she wondered what it would be like to be loved by Alain Duval as his wife must have been, to feel the sensuous mouth awakening responses, destroying defences and to be able to abandon oneself to the desires he would undoubtedly build up.

Frenziedly she pushed such thoughts away, her hand going to her throat as he looked up, his gaze momentarily holding hers.

'Are you all right?'

'Yes, fine. It's a little hot in here.'

'I hadn't noticed, but you do look a little flushed.' He gave the order to the waiter, again without consulting her and for once she was glad. Her brain was incapable of functioning on such a mundane level and when the food came she picked at the salad of tomatoes and felt his frown of disapproval as she did the same with the *Côte de Veau Maintenon*. It was beautifully cooked and presented, yet the delicate flavour of the veal and mushrooms were wasted on her. Everything tasted like chaff.

'I'm sorry, I suppose I'm just not really hungry after all,' she said lamely, in answer to his comment. 'It is rather late.'

He put his glass down and she purposely avoided the glittering look in his eyes. 'I appreciate your concern for your patient, but aren't you taking it a little too far?'

She blinked. What did he mean? She hadn't even been thinking of Gray. The fact that she hadn't made her feel slightly guilty.

'Of course I realise it is more personal than that. After all, he is the man you love.' His voice was icy, mocking, so cold that it took her breath away.

'Of course I'm worried. Don't I have the right to be?'

'Undoubtedly.' His mouth was taut. 'Any woman has the right to worry about the man who intends to marry her. Gray does intend marriage I suppose?'

Her heart thudded sickeningly as she tried to evade the deliberately cruel gaze. Was marriage what Gray had in mind? With a rising panic she realised that she didn't know, but how could she admit that to a man like Alain Duval?

'My personal feelings have nothing to do with this. In any case do you really imagine we've discussed such things at a time like this?' Her hands tightened. 'All I'm concerned with is seeing him get well again.' Her glance flew up. 'The tests . . . have you had the results?'

'As it happens, yes I have. That was what I wanted to talk to you about. I've decided to go ahead and operate.' His voice was curt and Clare felt her throat tighten.

'When?'

His hand moved fractionally against his glass. 'The sooner the better, for everyone's sake. At least then you'll be able to go ahead and make plans. I've decided to go ahead before the end of next week.'

What did he mean, plans? Why was he looking at her like that? 'So soon?' Her voice was hollow. Now that the moment had actually come she felt drained, afraid.

'I thought it was what you wanted.'

'Yes, of course it is. More important it's what Gray wants. It's been a kind of hell for him this past few weeks. But . . . what chance . . . how soon will we know if it has been a success?'

'A few days, when the bandages come off. As for the chances, you may as well know the truth, we could be lucky. He could regain his sight completely or he could end up with tunnel vision. That's something he would have to learn to live with. It's better than total blindness.'

'But his painting?'

'I wouldn't think he would be able to go on.'

She sat back trying to absorb it all, putting herself into Gray's shoes. How would he feel? 'And if it doesn't work?' She had to ask it.

'Then I can't do any more.' He was watching her. 'But I aim to do my damndest to see to it that it doesn't come to that.'

She believed it, just as she believed with absolute certainty that if anyone could help Gray, it was this man. She picked up her napkin, dabbing at her lips where the wine had left a sour taste and as she did so her gaze fell automatically on the figures seated at a table on the other side of the restaurant. Her brain numbly registered something familiar but it was several seconds before full realisation came and with it a feeling of incredulity, of betrayal almost, as she saw the woman laugh gently at the man seated opposite before the beautiful face turned and Clare felt as if the breath was being driven out of her lungs by some invisible force. She stared at

Gray. It wasn't possible that he should be here, of all places, and with Francine. With a gasp of disbelief which was almost a sob her gaze flew accusingly to Alain as the suspicion began to dawn on her that he had known, that he had done this deliberately.

His eyes met hers, blandly, and the words which flooded chokingly to her lips were stifled in her need to escape. It was his hand on hers which stopped her in mid-flight.

'I think we're about to have visitors.'

She had half risen to her feet but it was already too late. Gray and Francine were making their way slowly towards them.

'Well, well, this is a surprise. Miss Summers, Gray darling, here is your little nurse with the good doctor. I thought I must be mistaken but, *non*. How very nice for you both, enjoying a cosy little dinner together.'

Clare was aware of the colour flooding into her cheeks and of Alain, rising to his feet, smiling tautly up into the green eyes. 'Nurse Summers and I had a number of matters to discuss and as neither of us had eaten . . . It was strictly business.' He laughed, as if genuinely regretting the fact, but that wasn't possible.

Gray's expression was unreadable. She wished it wasn't. What Alain had said was perfectly true, it was strictly business, yet for some reason, hearing it said so coldly filled her with an inexplicable sense of depression.

'You don't need to explain.' Gray said, slowly now and almost with a hint of guilt. 'We finished earlier than planned at the exhibition hall and decided to eat out too.' He hadn't needed to explain. The fact that he did so made Clare wonder if it was entirely true. Judging from the triumphant gleam in Francine's eyes, it wasn't completely unplanned.

Clare rose to her feet. 'I think we had finished, Doctor.' She was discomfited to see him actually smiling at Francine, apparently quite satisfied with his evening's work.

'I think so. We've said all that needed to be said.'

'Ah, that is good.' The generously painted mouth smiled. 'I would not wish to have disturbed your meal.'

'You didn't.'

Clare felt her jaw tighten. All she wanted now was to get back to the château as quickly as possible, but he made no attempt to move and, incredibly, she heard him say, 'Perhaps I can give you a lift back to your apartment.'

'Oh but surely, Miss Summers . . .'

'Is quite capable of driving Gray back home, isn't that so?' He was looking at her and Clare ground her teeth together. 'Since you have to go back there anyway it seems a little pointless for her not to drive Gray and as I said, our business was finished.' It was galling to be dismissed so cold-bloodedly. 'You do have your car?' He was smiling at Francine.

'*Mais oui*.' She dangled the keys and Clare all but snatched them from the beautifully manicured fingers.

'Then that's settled.' His hand was under Francine's arm and she stood watching them disappear fighting back an angry wave of resentment before she remembered Gray.

'Well, we'd better go. The evening would appear to be over for both of us. I'm only sorry you'll have to put up with my driving and my company instead of Francine's.' She knew she sounded peevish but couldn't help it. Everything was going wrong, though in what way she couldn't have said. After all, she was with Gray, wasn't she?

'I'm not complaining. It would have been a little crazy for Francine to drive me home and Alain to take you in the same direction you must admit?'

Yes she had to admit it. The arrangement was perfectly logical but that didn't take away the rather nasty feeling that Alain had been in almost indecent haste to exchange her company for that of Francine. Not that she could blame him, she thought with a sigh.

CHAPTER TEN

THEY drove in silence back to the château, Clare concentrating on the road ahead, Gray resting his head back against the seat, his eyes closed. He looked tired—more than that, exhausted—yet she had the feeling he wasn't actually sleeping but watching her as if waiting for her to speak, or perhaps wanting to say something himself but waiting for the right moment.

Whatever it was, she couldn't help him. There seemed nothing to say. It had come as more of a shock than she had realised at the time, to see him enjoying what was obviously an intimate twosome with Francine. The fact that he was a perfectly free agent and had every right to be there didn't lessen the hurt even though she knew it to be unreasonable.

She sighed unconsciously and was glad as the car edged its way up the drive and came to a halt. She was tired and wanted to get to bed. The complexities which seemed to be tying her emotions into knots would have to wait. But having watched Gray climb out of the car he detained her when she would have said goodnight and hurried to her room.

'Stay and have a nightcap.'

She stood, gloves in hand. 'I'd rather not if you don't mind. I'm very tired, Gray.'

'I know,' he frowned, 'but I don't want to just leave it like this. I think we should talk, don't you?'

She stirred uneasily. 'There's not really much to say is there? It's not important.'

'I think it is. I want you to understand. Surely it's not asking too much that you give me a few minutes to explain.'

Clare sighed but turned reluctantly coming down the stairs again and following him into the library where he poured two drinks.

She took it even though she didn't want it. Brandy wasn't a drink she particularly liked, but her hand closed round the glass, glad to have anything which stopped herself shaking.

'I don't see that any explanations are needed,' she began.

'Did you enjoy your meal with Alain?'

The question took her by surprise. 'It wasn't exactly a social outing. He wanted to talk business.'

'Oh yes, of course. Discussing the patient while he isn't around.'

'It wasn't like that at all. We had neither of us eaten . . .'

'Clare, I really don't care.' His voice was curt. 'You're free to come and go as you please, I've told you that. In any case I can hardly say too much since you caught me in exactly the same situation with Francine.' He moved uneasily. 'We decided on the spur of the moment to go on and eat somewhere. You've no idea how much arranging the exhibition will take. We had a lot to talk about.'

'I'm sure you did,' she murmured, putting her

glass down untouched on the table. 'But as you said, you don't owe me any explanations either, Gray. You're free to do as you please. My concern is purely professional. You know you mustn't get over-tired.'

'Is that all?' His mouth had compressed. 'Just professional concern?'

She gasped as he gripped her arms. 'What else?'

'I'd rather imagined . . . hoped that it might be something more, that you might actually care for me, Clare. Or was I mistaken?'

She swallowed hard, feeling too tired to argue. 'Gray, what is it that you want of me?'

'Don't you know? I thought I'd made it clear.'

'Not to me. Or perhaps I'm being particularly obtuse.'

He was silent, a variety of emotions flickering over his face. 'Dear God, what a fool I've been. I was sure you must know what you mean to me.'

A strange restlessness came over Clare. Suddenly she wasn't sure she wanted this conversation to continue. 'How could I know? I was just a child when we first met. You scarcely noticed me. How could I possibly know what your feelings are?'

'You mean just because you happened to see me with Francine? But I've explained, that was business, nothing more.' He drew her towards him and kissed her roughly. 'My darling, you have no reason to doubt my feelings or to be jealous of Francine. Yes, I disobeyed your orders. I should have come home when our business was over, but

Francine is useful to me and I have to keep her happy, surely you can see that? She has contacts. Contacts I need.'

It sounded cold-blooded and vaguely distasteful. 'She is also very beautiful,' Clare heard herself say it. 'I wouldn't blame you . . .'

He shook her. 'You have no need to blame me because what I say is true, I want you, I need you. I just wonder . . .' he broke off, 'have I any right to ask you to care, knowing what may happen?' To her utter dismay he covered his eyes with his hand. 'Dear God, if only I knew what was going on, what sort of future I have. Until then, how can I ask you the things I want to ask? But if you can only wait until this nightmare is over.' She was in his arms and felt the tears on her own cheek. 'Be patient, my darling Clare. It can't be much longer.'

She returned his kisses, feeling his need of her and unable to bring herself to draw away.

'Oh Gray, Gray,' she leaned her head against him, then he raised her face, kissing her again.

She laughed unsteadily, brushing a hand through her hair. 'This isn't good for you. I'm your nurse. I'm supposed to see that you stay calm.'

'More than just my nurse.' He was reluctant to let her go and her heart missed a beat.

'Yes, but you've a lot ahead of you still. I was going to tell you, Alain is going ahead with the operation. That was what we were discussing this evening.'

His hands were rigid against her arms. 'When?'

'A few days. He'll let us know. Oh Gray, don't

look like that, it will be all right I know it will. It has to be.'

'Yes, it does, doesn't it?' He laughed uneasily and then, as she moved towards the door. 'You'll stand by me won't you, Clare.'

'You don't need to ask, you know I will.' She went up to her room leaving him to pour another brandy, spilling a little but unaware of it as he stood brooding in front of the fire.

Taking off her coat she began to unzip her dress and saw the faint bruises on her arms where Gray had held her. She still couldn't believe that he actually loved her, it was too much like a dream, a prayer suddenly answered. So why wasn't she feeling ecstatic, up in the clouds? After all it was what she wanted, wasn't it?

Her glance went to the photograph of Gray and Danielle, taken so long ago during that glorious summer she had spent at the château, the summer when she had first fallen in love, and a tiny dart of doubt began to tug at her mind as the features blurred and somehow became those of Alain Duval.

CHAPTER ELEVEN

THE call, when it came, seemed to bring a releasing of all the tensions which had been building up over the past few days, almost as if with the arrival of the moment of truth at last Gray accepted the inevitable and wanted only to get it over with.

Alain's voice had been coldly impersonal when Clare spoke to him. He had simply given her the time of Gray's admittance, a list of the things to bring in with him and asked for her notes. There was no mention of their evening together, no hint of an apology for the way he had ditched her in order to take Francine home she thought, as she slammed down the phone, and then realised that her anger was irrational. He had after all stressed that it was purely a business meeting, which made her sense of disappointment all the harder to understand.

Gray's operation however, pushed everything else from her mind. She drove him to the clinic and left him at the polite but firm insistence of the Sister in charge.

'Dr Duval wishes that his patient shall have no excitement before he performs the operation.' The attractive features studied Clare curiously. 'He left particular instructions that you were not to stay. I am sorry,' a hint of apology crept into her voice as

157

she saw the flush rise to stain Clare's cheeks.

She could hardly believe it, that he would go out
of his way to prevent her being with Gray just when
he needed her most. 'But I am a friend of Mr
Masterson's, as well as his nurse. Are you sure you
have Dr Duval's message correctly?'

The young woman consulted her notes. 'You are
Miss Summers?'

'Yes I am, but . . .'

'Then I am sorry but those are my orders.' She
frowned then smiled. 'As a nurse yourself I'm sure
you understand.'

Oh yes, Clare thought, grinding her teeth in
anger, she understood all right. Alain considered
her a bad influence and was deliberately keeping
her away from Gray, and there wasn't a thing she
could do about it.

She turned to leave then hesitated. 'I presume I
shall be able to see him after the operation?'

'Oh but yes, the doctor has given no orders to the
contrary, only that you should not stay now.' She
looked at her watch and smiled sympathetically.
'He is not meaning to be hard but sometimes it is for
the best. As a close friend you will worry and he
does not wish that you should do so, I am sure.'

Clare dug her hands into her pockets. 'I think I
understand the doctor's motives perfectly.'

'He will operate quite soon. It should be over by
this evening. Why do you not return then?'

It was pointless to argue and the galling part of it
was that Alain was probably right. It would serve
no useful purpose at all for her to remain worrying

about what was happening. It wasn't as if she could do anything for Gray. Her usefulness would begin afterwards . . . whatever the outcome.

But it wasn't so easy to fill in the rest of the day. She returned to the château but couldn't settle to anything somehow. In fact there was nothing to do now that Gray wasn't here and she wandered aimlessly from room to room, for the first time considering the future. If the operation was a success her job here would be finished and the realisation came as a shock. What would she do? Gray had asked her to wait, but for how long? She had to earn a living, at least until they were married. Uneasily she knew that everything was so vague. She stared down at the cup of coffee she held. It had gone cold but she drank it, grimacing and began to walk along the echoing galleries, peering into silent rooms. As Gray's wife this would be her home. It was beautiful but somehow unreal, she felt like a stranger, an intruder who had no right to be here, but surely that was ridiculous? Sighing, she returned to the library to sit before the blazing fire and watch the clock ticking the minutes away with nerve-shattering slowness.

It was late when she drove back to the clinic. Concentrating on her driving along the dark unfamiliar roads as well as the tension of waiting to hear about Gray had given her a headache and she was pale as she made her way towards Gray's room along the silent corridors.

This time she was admitted without question. 'Ah, Miss Summers, the patient came back from theatre a few hours ago so I'm afraid he won't be able to talk. He is still very dozy and Doctor has given him a sedative so that he will sleep well tonight. It is best if he moves as little as possible. But of course,' she smiled, 'you realise this. Please don't stay too long.'

'I won't.' Clare stood at the door, moving aside as the young woman left. Her gaze went to the bed where Gray lay motionless and fear stabbed momentarily at her heart. He looked so pale, so vulnerable? What if the worst should happen, would she be able to cope? Even if it didn't and the operation was a complete success, what then? Was she really the right wife for a man like Gray? She walked slowly to the bed, held by an odd reluctance. Why, all of a sudden, was her mind filled with so many doubts?

His eyes were bandaged, his hands lay on the covers, relaxed, sensitive hands. For some reason she found herself comparing them with Alain's, then pushed the thought away, sharply. If only the next few days were over putting an end to so many uncertainties.

She sat on the chair looking at Gray. It was some minutes later that she became vaguely aware of the door opening quietly behind her. It would be the nurse of course, come to tell her her time was up. She didn't look up until the voice beside her said, softly, 'He won't be awake properly for hours, not until morning. Why don't you go and get some sleep yourself. There's nothing you can do here.'

Dazed by tiredness she turned, taking in the

white coat before her eyes reached the drawn features above it. Alain repeated the words impatiently, as if to a child. 'Go home. There's no sense in
your hanging around here. He's certainly not going
to appreciate your concern, not yet, at least.'

It was as if he had struck her and she jerked out of
her daze feeling a slow return of anger. Before she
could say a word however his hand was on her arm
and she found herself steered out into the white
corridor with a speed which left her breathless.
Shaking him off she faced him.

'You used your authority to keep me away from
Gray this morning, don't try it again, Doctor. I
have every right to see him.'

He studied her in grim silence for a moment, a
dark frown gathering on his forehead. 'I used my
authority, as you put it, because it was in the best
interests of my patient. Not from any personal
motive.'

She laughed, shortly. 'Somehow I doubt that.
I'm not a fool, Doctor, I know you've never
approved of my relationship with Gray.'

'I'm not exactly sure what that relationship is, are
you, Miss Summers?'

She drew in a breath sharply. 'I don't see that it's
any business of yours.'

'No I'm sure you don't. But I'm making it my
business if it is going to affect my patient's progress.
I was also, in case it had escaped your notice,
thinking of you.'

Her eyes widened disbelievingly. 'Of me? I don't
understand.'

'No, I don't suppose you do, but what good would it have done if you had stayed? You would have been in the way. My staff have their own work to do and having to deal with hysterics isn't part of that job if I can possibly prevent it.'

Her eyes were brilliant with angry tears. 'I was not hysterical.'

'No? Well you're giving a pretty good impression of it now.'

It was true and she knew it, hating him for that perceptiveness which seemed to give him the ability to see into her soul. A stifled sob broke. She hadn't slept, hadn't been able to eat and her head ached. And now to be faced with his contempt was just too much. She turned away only to feel his hand clasp roughly over her arm.

'Wait,' he said, tersely, 'I'll take you home.'

'There's no need. I'm quite capable.' She tried to shake him off, but it was useless.

'Are you?' The steely eyes raked her white face. 'You little fool, you're in no state to drive anyway, but if it make you feel any better, don't get the idea I'm doing you any special favour, I was going out to the château anyway to see Danielle.'

She might have known, she thought bitterly. It was too much to expect that he could have had her own welfare at heart, but she hadn't the strength to argue. She waited numbly as he discarded his white coat and shrugged himself into a jacket then, wordlessly, he led her down the steps and into his waiting car.

He started the engine and it purred noiselessly

but he made no attempt to move. Instead he turned to study her in the semi-darkness and even though she couldn't see his features clearly she sensed the tension in him and it was vaguely frightening.

'You must love him very much.'

It was a statement rather than a question and as such required no answer, but would she have dared to attempt one anyway? Her hand rose, shakily to cover her eyes and she leaned back. In silence the car moved away and he didn't speak again until they drew up at the steps of the château, then he moved across her as if to open the door but making no move to do so.

She was aware of the faint smell of after-shave and antiseptic. Her eyes opened to find his face close to her own and she had to struggle with the sudden tightening in her throat.

'You need a good night's sleep.' His arm, along the back of the seat, was virtually supporting her and her gaze was drawn to the strong, masculine outline of his jaw. 'You're over-tired and there's still a long way to go before this is over. You're going to need your strength just as much as Gray. More so perhaps if I haven't done my job properly.' His mouth tightened as he looked at her. 'I hope to God you know just what you'll be taking on. But then, I don't suppose you even care, do you?'

Her hands shook with a strange, enveloping weakness which seemed to be robbing her entire body of the ability to move. Exhaustion was closing in like a great, dark wave so that when she opened her mouth to speak no words came. She burst into tears and with a strangled oath he took her in his arms. It was as if a door had opened and a hand had reached out, welcoming her into the warmth of a safe haven. She fell towards it, sobbing with relief.

'Don't, don't, my darling.'

The endearment didn't register any more than the grim look on his face before his mouth closed hungrily on hers. She made no attempt to resist, on the contrary, her lips responded as his kiss claimed her, gently at first until, as if sensing her own passion, it became demanding, ruthlessly drawing out emotions which, until now, she had vaguely imagined had been fulfilled. But it had never been like this, not with Gray, she had never felt the kind of magic she felt now, the heady breathlessness which set her head spinning.

In the close confines of the car his nearness was enhanced, like a drug. She didn't want to break away from the comforting warmth as he held her because she knew now that there was no escape from the truth. She was in love with Alain. It hit her like a physical blow, crazy and impossible. The words hammered over and over in her brain. The magic was all in her own mind. The interest he was showing in her now was nothing more than concern, pity. She was overwrought and he had comforted her, it was nothing more than that and she couldn't let it become more because Gray needed her and she had given him her word.

With a sob she jerked herself free and flung the car door open, almost falling out in her need to get away. The longer she stayed in his arms the harder it would become to remind herself of where her duty lay.

'Duty'. The word filled her with a sudden sense of horror. What had she done? As she closed the door behind her and stood leaning against it, it was some time before she heard the car's engine start up and drive away, leaving the night, still and empty and hollow. Only when he had gone did she run to her room to fling herself weeping on to her bed. Alain, it was Alain she loved, but it was Gray she would marry.

CHAPTER TWELVE

THE next few days were a nightmare which Clare managed to live through somehow. Luckily Danielle put her nerviness down to worry about Gray. It was something shared and understood but the visits to the clinic were hardest of all to bear.

On the day the bandages were due to be removed, Clare was there early. Anything rather than just sitting, waiting. Since the night when she had discovered the truth of her feelings for Alain she had hardly slept and knew that it showed in the whiteness of her face and the dark smudges beneath her eyes. She had gone over and over it in her mind as if it would change anything, but it hadn't. Only one thing was clear, if the operation had failed Gray was going to need her and there would be no question of her going back on her word. No matter what happened, she vowed that he would never suspect. He deserved better. Beyond that she couldn't bear to look. Her head ached with trying to find answers but there were none. The only certainty was that she loved another man.

Arriving at the hospital she was a little surprised to be asked by the Nurse who apparently recognised her from her previous visits, to wait.

'The doctor is with Monsieur Masterson now.'

A quiver of alarm ran through Clare. 'You mean he is actually removing the bandages.'

'*Oui.*' The nurse smiled. 'We could have some news very soon.' She moved away leaving Clare to pace the corridor, much as she had seen other anxious relatives do at St Mary's, but until now she had never quite realised the kind of tension they were suffering. She tried not to keep glancing at the closed door but the agony of not knowing what was happening was almost more than she could bear. In a way she was almost glad Danielle had decided to wait at the château for the verdict. The thought of having to hold any kind of conversation set her teeth on edge.

Standing at the window she stared out over the green slopes where the snow had virtually disappeared beneath the force of a pale, watery sun. It was difficult to imagine what it would be like here in the summer when the flowers were in bloom and the trees were heavy with leaves again. It was the kind of beauty which Gray as an artist would appreciate, if he was able to see it. Her hand tightened. 'Please, please God let the operation be a success. Let him see again.' Her heart drummed as she recognised in the prayer a release from her own torment. If the operation was a success she would go back to England, to her work. There were many nurses who devoted their lives to their work and were perfectly fulfilled. Not that her own life could be that, without Alain, but it would be better, fairer than marrying Gray under false pretences, and he would get over it. He would paint again and that had always been the real direction in his life. Summer, a time for healing. If only she could look into the future. But perhaps it was as well she couldn't.

The sound of her name being spoken brought her out of the reverie with a start and she looked up to see the nurse waiting.

'If you wish you may go in now, Miss Summers. The Doctor has given his permission. He feels that you should be present when the bandages are actually removed because of your special interest in the patient.'

There was a cruel irony to the words which bore down on her like a lead weight as, without speaking, she followed the girl into Gray's room. He was sitting on the bed, his face tense beneath the bandages which had been partially removed, and as if he had been waiting for her his hand went out, drawing her closer.

'Clare, is that you? Thank God you've come.'

At the other side of the bed, Alain's features tightened as he nodded briefly to the nurse.

'Right, let's get on with it shall we? I'm going to take it slowly, Gray. A little at a time until only the pads are left. When I remove those I want you to open your eyes gently. You may find everything is rather misty at first and there may be some soreness. Don't worry, that's all perfectly normal. And don't be afraid if your vision isn't one hundred percent. I don't expect it to be at this stage. It will come. You understand?'

Gray nodded. His lips were compressed into a thin line. 'Can't we just get on with it.'

Clare found herself staring into Alain's face. His

brows were drawn together, the line of his jaw set. She wondered if he was regretting what had happened that night, the momentary impulse when she had been at her most vulnerable but at this moment he was all professional. The only thing that mattered was Gray and she might have been a hundred miles away. Dumbly she averted her gaze, watching, trance-like as he began to unwind the bandages.

It was a laborious job. She willed him to go faster and knew that he couldn't. The large hands with their incredible gentleness had a hypnotic effect on her and it seemed an eternity before he straightened up and nodded to the nurse.

'Draw the curtains, Nurse. We don't want too much light.'

The girl obeyed, returning to stand beside the bed. Alain was removing the cotton wool pads and Gray's hands went to his eyes.

'Slowly now, slowly, and remember, don't expect too much too soon.'

'I've waited so long,' Gray's voice was terse. 'I'm scared. What if it hasn't worked?'

He had put into words their own fears and Clare saw the brief flicker of anxiety in Alain's eyes. 'Well, let's find out before we start to worry about that. There's every reason to suppose it should be a success.'

Clare felt her nails bite into her palms. 'Please, please.' The words were unspoken. In the semi-darkened room it was impossible to judge completely Gray's reaction as he stared at the wall and

then in the direction of her own ashen face. He
blinked and shook his head, then his voice rasped,
'It's no good. All I can see is a faint blur.' He
reached out, his fingers touching her face. 'Clare, I
know it's you but I can't see you properly. My God,
is this it? Is this all I'm going to have for the rest of
my life?'

She drew in an agonised breath, staring helplessly at Alain, pleading with him silently to do something, perform some miracle. He pushed her gently
aside and sat on the bed, shining a small torch into
Gray's eyes. For some minutes he concentrated in
silence.

'Close your eyes again and open them slowly.
That's right, now look at my hand, follow it.' He
shone the torch again. 'Look at Clare, tell me what
you see, what colour she is wearing.'

She stood stock still as Gray turned in her direction. There was a note of excitement in his voice as
he said, hesitantly, 'Blue, she's wearing blue.' He
laughed. 'I can see, darling, I can see.'

He pulled her towards him and they were both
close to tears, her own not only of joy but panic.
She had to stop things before they got out of hand.
Tell him. Everything was going to be all right, he
could see, all she had to do was tell him the truth.
But not now, soon, when he was stronger. He was
kissing her as if oblivious to the presence of anyone
else. Clare was just dimly aware of the look on
Alain's face before he hurried from the room. It
had been taut with disapproval and contempt, but
why? The question remained unanswered as Gray's

hands turned her face towards him and he kissed her again.

At the nurse's insistence she stayed only briefly and was ashamed of the feeling of relief as she slipped away at last. She felt drained. Worse, she felt trapped. It had been so easy to tell herself that all her problems would be solved if Gray regained his sight, but his reaction had suddenly swept all her certainty away and depression closed in like a black cloud.

The sight of Alain drew her to a halt. She had the feeling he must have been waiting for her as he barred her path.

'I wanted to see you before you go.'

'Oh yes.' Her heart lurched. Why didn't he just leave her alone?

'Just to put your mind at rest.' His eyes seemed to hold hers with a look she couldn't fathom. 'Gray's sight isn't perfect yet but it will be, given time. I shall want him to attend the clinic at regular intervals obviously so that we can keep a check on his progress, and I shall prescribe some drops which will help. But apart from that,' his eyes raked her face, 'I really see no reason why you should delay your plans to arrange the wedding. I'm sure you won't want to waste any time.'

Why was he speaking so coldly? It was like a knife twisting in an open wound. She could tell him the truth, that she had no intention of marrying Gray, but the thought of having to endure his contempt was more than she could bear. Instead, she forced herself to say, calmly. 'No, I don't suppose we shall, after all, there doesn't really seem any reason . . .'

'Then I wish you well. Perhaps I should say congratulations.' He dug his hands into his pockets and walked away as if the subject suddenly bored him and after a moment she made her way out to the car and drove back to the château in a daze of unhappiness.

It was a week later that Gray telephoned in person with the news that he was being discharged from the clinic the following day. She knew she should be glad, and she was, but somehow the obvious pleasure in his voice made her spirits sink. Perhaps it was because she hadn't been prepared for him to make the call himself. She had expected something more impersonal and it was almost as if he had reached out and bound her even more tightly to him.

'Hullo, Clare, great news. They're letting me out of here tomorrow, isn't that marvellous?'

She had to force a lightness into her own voice as she answered but all the time her hands were shaking.

'Oh yes, that's marvellous. You must be delighted. It's seemed an age.'

'Yes, I am. I can't wait to get back to familiar surroundings, to see them properly again, to see faces again.' There was a slight catch in his voice. 'These past weeks have seemed like a lifetime, you've no idea.'

'I think I have, Gray. At least I can imagine.'

'Can you?' There was a note of doubt. 'I wonder

if anyone who hasn't been through it can ever really understand what it is to lose your sight. Life suddenly loses whatever meaning it had. Suddenly you're faced with the prospect of starting all over again without any of the advantages you once had and always took so much for granted. It's hell, Clare and it makes you lash out like a drowning man for something . . . someone, to cling to. Have you any idea what I'm talking about, Clare?'

She couldn't speak. Her voice seemed to be trapped in her throat. He was making it harder with every word he spoke.

'Clare, are you still there?'

'What . . . oh yes. I was just . . . so pleased for you.'

'You sound quiet, preoccupied.'

'No, just relieved it's all over. It's been a nightmare for me too, you know.'

There was a long pause. 'Yes, I keep forgetting that. I'm a selfish brute. You've been marvellous. God knows how I'd have got through these weeks without you. I'll never be able to repay you, you know that.'

There was an awkwardness, a reserve in his voice which she had never noticed before. She put it down to embarrassment and laughed to make it easier for him.

'You don't even need to think about repaying me. I was only doing my job.'

'Ah yes, your job. My angel in blue.'

Now it was her turn to feel embarrassed. Suddenly everything seemed stilted, different. 'Look, let me know what time you can leave the clinic and I'll come and pick you up in the car.'

'No,' he said quickly. 'Don't do that. There's no point in you coming all this way. I've managed to arrange a lift.'

'Oh that's fine. Who? One of the staff?'

There was a sudden blurring of the sound and she had the impression he had turned away. 'Look, I have to go.' There was a hint of impatience now. She knew that patients shared a limited number of telephones and didn't want to delay him by arguing so she said simply, 'All right, Gray, I'll see you tomorrow. I'll look forward to it.'

Why had she said that? Simply to ease her own guilt because of her lack of enthusiasm? Putting the receiver down her hand lingered. In a way perhaps she should be glad, the sooner she saw him again the better because it looked as if she was just going to have to get used to the idea of being Gray's wife if that was what he still wanted. She pressed a hand to her head. There wasn't going to be any escape after all, not without deliberately hurting him and that was something she knew now she couldn't bring herself to do. All she could do was to make sure he didn't suffer for it and she would work hard at it. She could give him affection and loyalty and provide the sort of home which would be a background to the sort of life they would share together.

CHAPTER THIRTEEN

SHE was awake just before dawn, cold and exhausted, but there was no point in just lying in bed thinking. She got up and made coffee, sitting in the kitchen to drink it and watching daylight gradually make its grey appearance.

Danielle was up early too, and on her way out to see friends who were backing Gray's exhibition. She was pulling on her gloves as Clare walked into the room.

'I feel I should stay to welcome Gray home, but I know how he hates fuss. Anyway, I think I might be in the way just a little, don't you?' She smiled, meaningfully but Clare purposely chose to misunderstand.

'I expect he will be rather tired for a few days but he'll soon be back to normal again.'

'I'm sure he will, with a little help, *non*?' Danielle lifted a hand as she swept out of the door leaving Clare to help herself to more coffee. She couldn't eat, food would stick in her throat, but she wasn't hungry in any case. If only she knew what time to expect Gray, but there hadn't been time to ask and even if there had, she realised miserably that it wouldn't have made any difference. The inevitable had to be faced sooner or later.

Going up to her room she took herself to task for

her selfishness. It wasn't, after all, going to be easy
for Gray. He had gone through a lot and even
though the operation had been a success he had a
long way to go before he found and rebuilt his
confidence sufficiently to start painting again.
Naturally the exhibition would take on a new
meaning now. Whereas before it had given him
hope to carry on, now it would be a challenge, a
chance to prove to himself and to others that he had
the talent which so many people believed in. The
fact that he had chosen her to help him face the
challenge was frightening but she knew she
wouldn't let him down. His words came back to her
quite clearly. 'Wait until this nightmare is over.'
Well for Gray the nightmare was over and no
matter what happened she would keep to her side
of the bargain and make sure he was never hurt
again.

With a conscious effort she changed into a new
dress. The cowl neck brushed against her hair, its
colour seeming to emphasise the colour of her eyes.
The soft wool moulded to her figure, a belt neaten-
ing her slender waist, the skirts swinging lightly as
she moved. It looked good, she admitted it to
herself without false modesty.

She was just adding a trace of lipstick to her
mouth when she heard the car draw to a halt in the
drive below and just for an instant her hand shook.
The doors slammed and she heard voices, faintly,
but knew that even if she could bring herself to go
to the window to look, she wouldn't be able to see
from this room anyway.

She sat in front of the mirror, steeling herself to the moment when she would have to go downstairs. This was ridiculous. Why should it be so difficult? After all, Gray was a good, kind, attractive man. Marriage to him would be no disaster, far from it, and yet she knew now, when it was too late, that she had never really loved him, not in the true sense of the word. It had all been part of a dream, a dream which she had built up around him and it wasn't his fault if he hadn't lived up to the image she had created and which might have remained if it hadn't been for Alain Duval who had walked arrogantly into her life and taught her what real love was. But she must forget him now, put him out of her mind. Perhaps, some day, she would forget him altogether.

The decision was almost a relief, a relief which made her lift her head, fix a smile on her face and run lightly down the stairs to where Gray was waiting. Through the closed doors of the library she heard the muffled sound of voices, Gray's and another, probably whoever had driven him home.

She walked into the room and saw Gray standing before the fire. He looked well. The tautness was gone from his face and he was smiling as she ran to his arms, determined to begin now as she meant to go on.

'Gray, oh Gray. It's lovely to have you home again.' She kissed his cheek and smiled up at him and it was some seconds before she realised that he wasn't responding, that he was holding her, stiffly, awkwardly and without a similar pleasure. His glance went over her shoulder and as Clare's eyes searched his face, a voice drawled softly from behind her.

'Well, well, how very touching. The poor girl has obviously missed you, darling.'

Clare whirled round to gaze with horror into Francine's amused face. The beautiful lips were smiling but it was the fact that her eyes smiled too which made Clare's heart lurch. What was happening? Why was she here, now of all times? Then, as she watched, Francine moved casually, placing her arm through Gray's to stand beside him and Clare's gaze fixed rigidly upon the diamond which glittered cruelly on the beautifully manicured left hand.

She couldn't believe it. There was some explanation of course. Her mouth felt dry as her gaze flew to Gray's face, seeing the embarrassment there, and only then did realisation truly begin to dawn and a feeling of sickness began to gather in the pit of her stomach. It was a joke, it had to be joke. She drew back, incapable of speech. She wanted Gray to put it into words, her gaze pleaded with him silently and she wondered why she had never noticed until now the weakness of his jaw, or the way he avoided looking at her directly.

It was Francine who broke the silence. 'Darling, I do think you should tell Miss Summers our good news. I'm sure she must have suspected anyway.'

He smiled, sheepishly then it faded. 'Yes, well I don't quite know how to put it.'

'Why not try "we're getting married", darling.

The simplest way is always the best, don't you agree, Miss Summers?'

Clare stared, dumbly. Incredibly she didn't know whether to laugh or cry as she looked at Gray, waiting for his confirmation and seeing it in his eyes even before he spoke. His hand rested almost defiantly over Francine's. Clare wondered vaguely whether he imagined she might create a scene but even had she been capable of it, nothing was further from her mind.

'Congratulations,' she heard herself say and somehow she even managed to smile. Suddenly she felt cold and sick. How had it happened? How could she have been so wrong? Her glance rose to his face. Or had she? Her brain, battling with confusion reminded her that Gray had never actually spoken about marriage. It had been implied, or again, perhaps she had merely believed what she wanted to believe when he had asked her to wait, when he had said he needed her. In the space of a few minutes she had been made to see that she had been a fool.

'I'm sure you'll be very happy.' Her mouth ached from smiling. 'When is it to be?'

'Soon.' He glanced at Francine. 'Before the exhibition we hope. Francine has put in such a lot of hard work. It seems right that she should share the glory as well.'

'Yes, of course.'

'You'll come to the wedding won't you?' Francine smiled triumphantly. 'After all, you've been such a help to Gray during these past few weeks. He's told me how you've put up with his moods, but now that will be my job, won't it, darling?'

Clare was already making for the door. The only thing she wanted was to get away. 'I'd like to, but I don't think I shall be here. My job is finished so it's time I was going back to England, after all I still have a job waiting for me.' She fought to keep her voice even. 'I've enjoyed being here but it's time I got down to some real work again. For Gray's sake I'm glad it turned out to be sooner than later.' She was sickened by the look of relief in his eyes and she closed the door quickly before he could say anything which would make things worse. Running to her room she sat on the bed and stared dazedly round her.

How could she have been such a fool? Gray hadn't needed her except as a prop during those weeks when he had been afraid and alone. But she realised now that he would have turned to anyone. It just happened that fate had cruelly chosen just that moment to bring her along and for her it had been as if a dream of years had been re-kindled.

It hadn't, she knew that now. She had never really loved Gray. What she had loved was an idea, a child's idea of how the world should be, full of happy ever afters but it hadn't worked out like that. She didn't want to be part of Gray's world and, tragically, the one she did want was gone. Alain believed she was in love with Gray, not that it mattered. She got to her feet and crossed to the window. He had made it perfectly clear that he had no interest in her whatsoever, and how could she blame him?

CHAPTER FOURTEEN

DRESSING quickly, Clare put the finishing touches to the packing she had begun the day before. Once her decision to leave was made it became a driving force. The sooner she got away for ever and started to pick up the threads of her old life the better. It wasn't going to be easy, she knew that, nothing could ever be quite the same again. The business with Gray, that was already beginning to take on the aura of a bad dream which had left nothing more than a bad taste in her mouth. But the rest? At the moment she couldn't bring herself to believe she would ever get over it. Her work would help of course if she threw herself into it heart and soul, gave herself no time to think. Perhaps eventually there might come a day when she wouldn't even think of Alain, feel the pressure of his lips on her own. Her hand strayed up to her mouth then she drew herself up quickly, brushing away tears. Why torture herself like this for a man whose only feeling when he learned that she had gone would be relief?

Looking at her watch she realised with a pang of alarm that if she was going to get to the airport by car in time she had better say goodbye to Gray. She had been putting it off purposely until the very last minute. The less they had to say to each other the better, she thought, ruefully, as she made her way downstairs and entered the library where he was working on some brief pencil sketches.

He looked up as she stood in the doorway and rose awkwardly to his feet. Studying him Clare realised with a slight sense of shock that he wasn't really attractive at all. His hair line was already beginning to recede and in a few years he would probably be overweight, but Francine wouldn't mind, as long as she had the glory of being the wife of a famous artist and Clare didn't doubt that Gray would be famous one day, provided he didn't make the mistake of living upon one success. Generously she hoped he did succeed and the hope was mirrored in her eyes as she held out her hand.

'I've come to say goodbye.'

He took it, making no attempt to release her. 'So soon?'

'I'm catching the evening flight. By morning, with a bit of luck, I shall be back on duty at St Mary's.' She laughed. 'I doubt if I've even been missed.'

His lips formed an answering smile then it faded as he studied her features as if seeing them clearly for the first time. 'You'll be missed here too, Clare, I want you to know . . .'

'Don't, Gray.' Jerkily she withdrew her hand. 'There's nothing to be said. You'll be married in a few weeks time and I know you're going to be happy. Francine will make a good wife.'

His mouth tightened sullenly. 'There's no reason

for you to rush away. I'm going to need some nursing for a while yet.'

'Not real nursing.' She was surprised to feel a spark of anger at the note of self-pity in his voice. 'Yes, you'll have to visit the clinic, but they can deal with you now. There's really nothing more I can do, Gray, and you should be pleased.'

He caught at her arm. 'Couldn't I persuade you to stay.' For a moment she stared at him thinking she must have misheard. 'Just because I'm married needn't make any difference,' his voice was softly persuasive. 'You understand what I'm saying, Clare? I've always had a soft spot for you.'

With a gasp she pulled away, fighting the nausea which rose in her stomach as she looked at him. Oh yes she understood all right, only too well, and the thought sickened her. Gray was weak and always would be.

'No, I'm sorry, Gray, you can't persuade me, not any more so please don't try. I'm leaving as soon as the car comes round.' She freed herself from his grasp. 'I've already said goodbye to Danielle, so if you don't mind I have a few more things to pack in my case.' She left him standing there and couldn't bring herself to look back as she closed the door quickly behind her, shutting him from her view for the last time.

Back in her room she flung the rest of her belongings carelessly into the suitcase and locked it. Wheels crunched on the drive below, the car come to take her to the airport. In a few hours she would be home. Home and alone. But it was best not to think about that now.

Shrugging herself into her coat she gave one last glance round the room, picked up her suitcase and went downstairs. Outside in the snow she stood on the steps looking in dismay for the car she had been expecting, but it wasn't there. In its place was another, one she recognised only too well and a knot of apprehension tightened in her stomach. Determinedly she ignored it. She hurried down the steps, her grip tightening on the handle of her suitcase but it was too late. The tall figure was already unwinding himself from the front seat and coming grimly towards her.

A sob choked in her throat as Alain's hand closed roughly over her arm and with the other he jerked the case from her grasp, dropping it to the ground as he spun her angrily to face him.

'And just what do you think you're doing?' His hand gestured towards the luggage and her mouth tightened.

'I'm leaving. I would have thought that was pretty obvious even to you.' Her head jerked upwards. 'I'm sure you're pleased, you never exactly approved of my association with Gray did you, Doctor?'

He stared at her and she saw the confusion which clouded his eyes. 'I don't understand a word you're saying. What the devil's going on?' His hand tightened again making her wince. 'Leaving? But I just heard about your engagement.'

Her heart was pounding wildly in her rib-cage. 'My engagement?'

'The word's all over the clinic.'

She laughed brittly. 'Then I'm afraid the word is wrong, Doctor.'

'You mean you're not engaged?'

'I really don't see how much plainer I can make it, but no, I'm not. Oh yes, Gray *is* engaged, to Mademoiselle D'Aubigne, so you can save your congratulations, I know how insincere they would be. I take it that is why you came, to tell me I wasn't good enough for Gray, well he saved you the trouble.' She was close to tears as she tried to free herself from his grasp. Thrusting him aside she tried to reach her suitcase. 'If you'll excuse me I'm late already.'

'And just where are you going?' he demanded, harshly.

'If you must know I have a plane to catch, if you'll let me go.' She looked frantically at her watch now, but to her dismay he made no attempt to release her, instead his hands were on her shoulders and he jerked her roughly to him forcing her to drop the suitcase heavily. His face was taut and she felt a quiver of fear.

'Before you go anywhere I want to get something straight. You say Gray is engaged to Francine?'

'Yes. I'm sure you'll be able to read about it in all the best society papers if you don't believe me.'

He shook her angrily. 'I do believe you. What I find hard to take is your indifference. For God's sake, don't you care?'

Her gaze rose slowly to meet his. 'No, not particularly. As a matter of fact I think he and Francine

are admirably suited and I wish them joy of each
other.' She laughed. 'Actually, you were right,
Doctor when you said that I was a child playing at
adult games. I was doing just that. But suddenly
I've grown up. I realise now what a fool I've been. I
don't love Gray, I doubt if I ever really did. What I
loved was an idea, a dream, but like most dreams
the ending wasn't the one I imagined it would be.'

He was staring at her, hard. 'But what about
Gray, he was in love with you?'

'No, I don't think so, Doctor, I think he simply
liked the idea of having someone adore him. It
amused and flattered him. Now,' her fists clenched,
'can I go. I really don't see that we have any more to
say.' She was stiff in his arms. The feel of his hands
was making her heart behave crazily again and she
couldn't bear it if she broke down now. 'Please, let
me go.'

She expected him to release her but instead his
grip tightened and she felt herself jerked ruthlessly
closer until he was staring down into her eyes. His
mouth was close, so close that her lips ached with a
need to be possessed and she closed her eyes,
moaning softly.

'You're not the only one who's been a fool.' His
voice was gruff and, incredulously she felt his hands
move to stroke her hair and her cheeks.

'Wh . . . what do you mean?' As she stared up at
him a few flakes of snow settled in her hair. 'I don't
understand.'

'No, I don't suppose you do. I'm not sure that I
do completely either. I only know that when I

thought you were actually going to go ahead and marry Gray I knew I couldn't bear it. That's why I came here, to stop you, somehow, anyhow, to beg you not to go through with it because I love you.'

She felt dazed, as if none of what was happening was real. 'But . . . you can't. What exactly are you saying?'

'That I love you,' he repeated, 'and you're going to marry me.'

She shook her head. 'But it isn't possible.'

'Why not?' He seemed to be laughing at her now.

'Because . . . because since the first moment when we met you've made it perfectly clear that you disapproved of me, both as a nurse and as a wife for Gray.'

He kissed her mouth gently. 'In the latter case you're perfectly right.' His lips moved to her chin. 'I was so damned angry I admit I may have been a little unreasonable.'

'Unreasonable.' She choked and was kissed again. 'You were abominable, arrogant.'

'I know and I can't promise I'll ever change. Each time I see you look at another man I shall probably be the same, but once you're my wife I shall feel safer.'

'Aren't you rather taking things for granted?' She protested, weakly. Things were getting out of hand. He was taking over again. 'I'm leaving for England in . . . oh no, half an hour.'

'You'll never make it,' he said, and there was laughter in his eyes. 'So why don't we drive somewhere nice and quiet and make some plans?'

'What sort of plans?'

'Oh, like where we shall live, how many children we want. When you'll meet my mother. You'll love her. She'll love you.'

'Haven't you forgotten something?'

He frowned. 'I don't think so.'

'We haven't fixed a date for the wedding yet. I haven't even said I'll marry you.'

'But you will and I've already fixed the date. Next week will be fine and that's an order, Sister.'

She would have protested, half-heartedly, but he silenced her with a kiss and suddenly she didn't feel like arguing any more.

Doctor Nurse Romances